SLEEPLESS

For Oliver, who isn't afraid of anything...

STRIPES PUBLISHING LTD
An imprint the Little Tiger Group
1 The Coda Centre, 189 Munster Road,
London SW6 6AW

www.littletiger.co.uk

This paperback edition first published in Great Britain in 2015

ISBN: 978-1-84715-455-2

Printed and bound in the UK.

10 9 8 7 6 5 4

SLEEPLESS

LOU MORGAN

RED EYE

Chapter One

"Just a few more weeks. That's all – a few more weeks and then we're done."

"Until September."

"Whatever."

"And, you know, aren't you forgetting something? Like exams, maybe?"

Everyone else groaned, despite Grey's grin. Nobody needed (or wanted) to be reminded about the exams. The Clerkenwell School took exam results very seriously indeed. Almost as seriously as their parents did.

The bell signalling the last of the afternoon's classes rang, and Izzy hauled herself up from the small grass square that passed for the Clerkenwell's courtyard, dusting down her school skirt and scooping her bag on to her shoulder. All around the courtyard, students started towards their respective classrooms, watched from the doorways by the school prefects. Not that anyone was in much of a hurry – it was the last real day of term. When the bell rang at 3:30pm, that was it. Study leave – and then exams, yes, but Izzy wasn't going to think about that until she had to. Which was horribly soon.

If she was honest, she thought, hitching the strap of her bag further over her shirt, it was *probably* about three weeks ago. Mia and Dom had had their revision timetables all drawn up and printed out by half term. "Tiger mother," they'd said in unison when Noah had sniggered at the neat charts marked up in the twins' diaries – everyone knew how pushy she was when it came to school. Not that Noah had much to worry about. He was probably the only one of the whole group who stood a chance of getting anywhere near a top grade. There was a reason he was at Clerkenwell, after all, and unlike most of them it wasn't his family's money.

Izzy slipped into her seat in the English classroom just ahead of Kara and Grey. Kara kept her head down – she was the one person in the whole class who looked unhappy about the end of term. It didn't exactly take a genius to know why, either. Poor Kara. She was so afraid of being on the outside that she'd rather be the butt of Tigs's jokes than risk being forgotten. You could see it in her face. Even after all the time she and Tigs had known each other, she was still afraid of being shut out. All she wanted was to be part of this mythical 'inner circle' that had Tigs at its centre. Izzy had said as much to Grey, not all that long ago, as they'd waited for the lifts in the lobby of the Barbican's Lauderdale Tower where they both lived.

Grey had shrugged and said, "You know what else has an inner circle? Hell."

"You're telling me Antigone Price is the devil?" Izzy had laughed as the lift pinged and the doors opened, following Grey inside. She'd jabbed the button for the thirteenth floor, followed by the eighteenth for him.

"Maybe not the devil. But she comes pretty close…"

The afternoon dragged. Nobody bothered to hide the fact they weren't working, and even their teacher didn't seem too concerned. Mrs Alderman went as far as to sit down, tell them all to read a book and to get out a magazine for herself. She flipped through it, occasionally glancing up to make sure they were at least all still there.

A fly buzzed inside the sash window beside Izzy's desk, somehow trapped between the two panes of glass. On the other side of the window, she could just make out the top of Lauderdale Tower looming over the neighbourhood.

When they first met, living in the Barbican had been her way in with Tigs – who had apparently decided that everyone living within the confines of the Barbican estate's walls was (in her words) 'safe'. Everyone *outside* was not. It was a ridiculous idea given that an apartment across the road in Florin Court – where Kara lived – cost just as much as one in the Barbican's blocks and had its own residents' pool, but that was Tigs all over. It wasn't just about the money – although money was definitely a part of it. It was about something more. Of course, Tigs still hadn't let Izzy forget that she was a new girl. She'd only moved in a year ago, hadn't she? Tigs had been *born* there.

With its locked residents' garden and its lake with fountains and terraces, the Barbican was a maze of low-rise blocks punctuated by three towers. Sitting at the edge of the bustling City of London business district, just behind St Paul's Cathedral, it had been built on land flattened by the bombs of the Blitz. The idea was that it would be the future of city life – thousands of flats and apartments in all shapes and sizes, raised up above the level of the roads and the traffic below. It was intimidating from the outside, designed to look almost like a castle. Even its name, Barbican, meant a kind of fortress. In the middle was the garden and the lake, and the Barbican Centre itself – a complex of theatres and cinemas, art galleries, libraries and restaurants open to the public, provided they could find the entrance. The whole place was a labyrinth of different levels, walkways that led nowhere and doors that could only be opened with a resident's key. It was 'exclusive'. And Tigs lived in the most exclusive part – a sprawling apartment on the thirty-fifth floor of Shakespeare Tower, one of the high-rise blocks right at the heart of it. Something she liked to remind *everyone* of at every possible opportunity.

A loud scraping sound, followed by a crash, snapped Izzy's attention away from the window and back into the room. Two rows ahead of her, a chair was lying on its side in the aisle and next to it Grey was flat on his back, crying with laughter. Mrs Alderman peered over the top of her magazine, scowled and shook her head. It wasn't the first time Grey had managed to fall off his chair in class. He bowed to the room – obviously enjoying the applause he was getting – and picked up his seat, dropping back down into it with a grin.

"Show-off," Izzy muttered.

When the bell rang, finally, she hung back, sliding her folder carefully back into her bag. Mrs Alderman had moved on to the crossword, and as Izzy passed the teacher's desk, she glanced up. "Murder, Izzy?"

"How many letters, Mrs Alderman?"

"Eight."

"Homicide, Mrs Alderman. But you know that already."

"Just testing." Mrs Alderman tapped her pen on the magazine. "How's the revision going?"

"It's going." Izzy made what she hoped was a non-committal sound.

"You are taking it seriously, aren't you?" The teacher was suddenly stern. "I'm not trying to pass judgement, but after your last school I know how important—"

"I'm taking it seriously. I am. Honestly." Izzy stared at the floor. The classroom suddenly felt like it was shrinking, getting smaller and smaller. The walls were pressing in on her and all she could think about was getting out.

"I'm glad to hear it. These exams could affect your whole future. This isn't a dry run, this is the real thing." She blinked at Izzy, watching her reaction – then said, more kindly, "Although that's not to say you shouldn't have a break now and then."

"No, Mrs Alderman."

The teacher looked her up and down. "Go on, then. I imagine your friends are waiting for you. Tell Grey I look forward to seeing his exam script, by the way…"

"I will, Mrs Alderman." Izzy smiled, and clutching her bag tightly she headed out of the classroom and into the bright sunlight of the courtyard.

Exactly as predicted, Grey was waiting, along with the others, on the grass. Izzy came out just in time to see him drop to his knees, shouting "Freedom!" at the top of his voice. His school tie was clutched in one of his raised fists and his dark hair flopped across one of his eyes.

"You're such a loser," she said, stopping just in front of him.

"You love it," he grinned up at her, brushing his hair out of his face. "It makes you feel superior."

"I am superior. Obviously."

"You keep telling yourself that." Grey shook his head.

"So, I was thinking," said another voice from somewhere behind Izzy's head, cutting through their conversation as though it wasn't happening. Her heart sank. Tigs. She didn't turn round, hoping that Tigs would take the hint. Some hope – Tigs carried on regardless.

"I was thinking – revision party? My place? Later?"

"Revision party? Yeah, right. Like my parents will go for that," said Juliet, perched on the wall next to Dom. She peered over her sunglasses at Tigs.

"Fine. 'Study group', then." Tigs sighed theatrically. "Aren't they working, anyway?"

"Mum's on the rota, Dad's on call. Go figure."

"What they don't know while they're busy being super-doctors won't hurt them, will it?" Tigs flicked her glossy blonde hair back over her shoulder and beamed. "So it's sorted. Six o'clock."

"Shall we even bother bringing books?" Noah raised an eyebrow at Tigs, who pouted.

"Depends if you want to waste time studying, doesn't it?" With another hair flick, Tigs shot them all a dazzling smile and flounced off in the direction of the main entrance, forcing Noah to step out of her way. If Grey noticed the sway of her skirt as she went, he didn't show it. But then, he never did. Dom, on the other hand…

Juliet followed his gaze. "Ugh. You're all so predictable."

"Shh." Dom tried to put his hand over her mouth. "No talk. Pretty girl walking."

"Oh, come off it!" Juliet twisted underneath his arm and gave him a gentle shove. He slipped backwards on the wall and only saved himself from going over altogether with an undignified scramble.

"You know that was all for you, don't you?" Izzy nudged Grey in the ribs as they fell into step. Their little group was the only one still in the courtyard.

Ahead of them, the solid wooden door on to the street stood open, while behind them Dom tried to empty the dregs of his water bottle over Juliet, who screamed and raced past them with Dom and Noah in hot pursuit, laughing. It was just the two of them left now. Grey watched the others for a moment as they ran off, then shook his head.

"Not interested."

"In Tigs? Doesn't look like she feels that way about you…"

"Yeah, well. I'm taken, aren't I?"

"What? Oh, in your *dreams*, lover-boy."

It had become a running joke – ever since the day she'd almost collided with him in their building's entrance lobby and seen the stack of terrible horror movie DVDs in his hands. Top of the pile was a copy of *Warlock*, of which she knew every single line. The bond had been instant, and since then they'd had regular horror 'dates' (as Tigs liked to call them, making little quote marks in the air with her fingers each time) watching endless schlocky films full of monsters, vampires and chainsaw-wielding maniacs. Grey liked the monsters – even if he got annoyed when Izzy pointed out that you could usually see

14

the seams in the swamp-creature's latex suit. Izzy, on the other hand, liked the serial-killer ones best, and it drove her crazy that Grey always guessed the bad guy. Any time Izzy shrieked or hid behind her hands, he would shrug and laugh smugly. "You knew that was coming though, right? If they die offscreen, they're not really dead." This was usually the point where she threw a cushion at him.

Grey and Izzy walked side by side on the narrow pavements, as they did every school day. In the mornings, the huge concrete bulk of the Barbican fell away behind them like a shadow. In the afternoons, it rose up to meet them. Today, it baked in the sun beating mercilessly down on the glittering skyscrapers of the City. To an outsider, looking at it from the wrong side of the forbidding wall, surely you'd have to be crazy to want to live there. It was hot in the summer and miserably gloomy in the winter, when the rain streaked the endless grey with black. But when you got into the middle of it (*if* you got into the middle of it) the Barbican was another story altogether. The garden was full of spreading trees that cast shade on even the hottest afternoons, and from inside the fence that kept the general public out, you could sit on the side of the lake and dangle your feet into the water.

The porter in the entrance hall of Lauderdale Tower nodded in greeting as they walked in, then turned back to whatever he was watching on the little television under the security desk. Grey ducked ahead through the glass doors into the lift lobby, flicking at the 'call' button on the central console, which sat on top of a small column in the middle, and turning to watch the three lifts expectantly.

"Which one, then?" he asked.

"I'm not playing." She tried to sound stern, but couldn't. They'd been playing this game ever since they'd started walking to and from school together last autumn, betting on which lift would arrive at the entrance level first.

"Come on. I'm going with … number three." He pointed his finger at the nearest lift. Sure enough, there was a sudden whirring sound from behind the closed doors and the little red floor indicator set above them began to count down the floors from twenty-five.

"Nah," she gave in. "It's almost four o'clock. You know what that means…" She held up her hands in triumph as the indicator lurched to a halt at seventeen.

"Mrs Johnson. Foiled again by the blue-rinse brigade."

Grey slumped dramatically over the centre console, dropping his bag on the floor. Every day at 4pm, little Mrs Johnson emerged from her apartment on the seventeenth floor to walk her poodle around the garden. The fact that dogs were allowed in neither the garden nor the actual apartments had never stopped her.

"Two. It'll be lift number two."

A moment later, lift number two pinged and the doors clattered open. Grey snatched his bag up from the floor and pouted at her.

"Next time, Whedon."

"You just hate losing. Admit it." She laughed as she pressed the buttons for their respective floors, and was still shaking her head at him when the lift stopped to let her out at the thirteenth.

"You want me to wait for you later?" Izzy pressed one hand against the side of the door to stop it closing.

Grey shook his head. "Nah. Go on over without me. My beloved mother's actually home so I'd better make nice."

"No party tonight? What's she going to do with herself?" Grey's mother had an incredibly successful party-planning business, but it meant that she spent most of her time going up and down the country overseeing the lavish events she'd organized. Grey didn't exactly say it out loud, but Izzy always got the feeling he resented all the travelling and the time she spent away from home.

"Probably try to organize *me*." Grey sighed. "I'll see you over there."

"Tigs'll sulk if she thinks you aren't coming…"

"Tigs will always find *something* to sulk about. I'm way down the list." He suddenly focused on a point just above Izzy's shoulder, and she turned round to follow his gaze. On the wall opposite, the floor indicator for lift number three whizzed through thirteen and on down to the lobby. Grey shook his head sadly and bit his lip. "Mrs Johnson…" he said sorrowfully as Izzy stood back, letting the doors slide shut.

"Where's Grey?" These were the very first words out of Tigs's mouth when she opened the door and

18

found Izzy standing on the other side. Alone. She blinked out at the landing, obviously expecting him to appear out of thin air.

"He said he'd come later." Izzy tried not to sound offended. "We're not joined at the hip."

"Whatever." Tigs quickly lost interest and flung the door wide open for Izzy to step through. "You're sure he's coming, though. Right?"

"Why don't you call him and ask *him*?" Izzy really was trying. She was.

"God, no. I'm not *calling* him. Besides, you usually know where he is. What's with you two, anyway?"

"Exactly the same as last time you asked me. Nothing."

"Like I said, whatever." Tigs held up a hand and kicked the door shut again.

In Izzy's apartment, the door would have slammed, shaking the whole floor. In the Price apartment, however, things worked a little differently. Their front door swung silently on its hinges, slowing down until the latch met the doorframe with a discreet, but solid, *click*. On the other side, the floor to ceiling windows of the living room took in the whole of the London skyline from thirty-something storeys up, the glass towers of the City glittering in the evening sun. On the vast red velvet sofa that dominated the room, Izzy could see Juliet and Mia, while Kara and Dom sat on the floor on the other side of the glass coffee table. There were, somewhat surprisingly, folders and notebooks open on the table.

"You actually *meant* 'study party', then?" Izzy jerked her head towards the revision notes.

Tigs looked blank, then laughed. "As if. It's in case the Paternal puts in an appearance."

"Your mum's not home?"

"She's on retreat."

"Is she OK?"

"The Maternal? Please. She treats that place like a hotel." Tigs breezed past Izzy and into the kitchen, pulling open the door to a fridge that was taller than either of them. "She'll be fine as soon as they dry her out. No. Wait." She slammed the fridge shut again and leaned back against the door, thoughtfully tapping the top of the drink she'd just pulled out. "They don't dry you out when it's pills, do they? What *do* they do? Shake you?" She stared into the middle distance, then shrugged. "Anyway, speaking of pills…"

There was a series of rapid knocks on the door. Tigs rolled her eyes. "It's open!"

"It's so not…" Grey's voice was muffled by the heavy wood and Tigs almost fell over herself in her rush to get to the door. It was either incredibly sweet or really pathetic – Izzy couldn't quite decide which.

However, Grey wasn't alone on the landing, which meant that Noah was treated to the full force of Tigs's best smile, as Grey breezed past her and threw himself down into an enormous armchair covered with a shimmering silvery fabric. In his torn jeans and his beaten-up Converse, he should have looked totally out of place, but there was something about him that said he *belonged*. It was easy for him, for Tigs … for all of them. All of them except for Izzy, anyway – and maybe Noah – and she felt almost jealous. Even Kara seemed to fit in here – she and Tigs had started school on the same day and as far as Izzy could tell, they'd been friends ever since. Well. Perhaps 'friends' was too strong a word for it, but there was definitely something there. Something that Izzy wasn't sure she'd ever have with Tigs, or with the others. Thinking about it like that, maybe Grey *was* the odd one out. 'Odd' being the operative word.

"Right. So. School's out. Monster exams coming up ... anyone else had 'the speech' yet?" Grey glanced around the room.

"Back in December," chorused Dom and Mia.

Grey blinked at them. "Your mum doesn't muck about, does she?"

"No."

"'I'm not worried about you disappointing me.'" Grey's impersonation of his mother was uncanny – even down to the way he moved his hands as he spoke, his fingers fluttering from side to side. "'I'm worried about you disappointing *yourself.*' It's like there's a book they get this stuff from."

"Exams, though." Squeezed into the middle of the sofa, Juliet looked a lot younger than everyone else, her eyes wide and earnest behind the thick frames of her glasses. "They're a big deal. I mean, if we don't do well in these..."

"Spare me." Grey's voice had an edge to it. "I got all this earlier."

"Maybe they're right. That's all I'm saying. We should take this stuff seriously." She was twirling her long pendant necklace around her finger, the way she always did when she was nervous. It was

22

a red glass bead, stretched into a teardrop the size of her thumb. Juliet never took it off. At school she wore it over her collar and tucked underneath her tie, and no matter how many times the teachers had threatened to confiscate it, they never had.

"Fine. But does everybody have to keep going *on* about it? Like that's going to help! It's not like we've never sat exams before, is it? We're Clerkenwell students. That's what we do."

"Not like these, though..."

"Juliet? Do me a favour? Stop talking, yeah?"

Their exchange had soured the mood in the room, taking it from celebratory to tense in less than a minute. Grey had said what the rest of them were already thinking, and Juliet had come a little too close to voicing everything that they were afraid of. They were Clerkenwell students, Grey'd been right about that. Their parents were successful. Their school was successful. They had no choice but to follow suit. Failure, at anything, was not an option.

It was Tigs who broke the silence. She was standing in the doorway, holding a small white paper bag. "As I was saying. I might be able to help with the whole ... revision thing." She rummaged in the bag and pulled out a stack of white oblong packets, tossing them to each of the group in turn.

The box rattled slightly as it landed in Izzy's hands. It was made of thick, glossy cardboard, embossed with the words *FokusPro* in heavy bold lettering. Nothing else. Inside were three silver blister-strips of tablets, shining in the light. They felt cold to the touch as she shook them into her hand, almost as though they were sucking the heat from her skin.

"You can thank me on results day," said Tigs smugly. "They're the new thing in the States. All the college kids are taking them for finals."

"A study drug?" Noah stared at the box resting on his palm. "Are you sure that's a good idea? Won't we get in trouble?"

"It's fine. I swear. They're just a bunch of vitamins and supplements or something. They're meant to help you work for longer, remember stuff better. All that. And it's not like anyone's going to *know*, is it?"

"Where'd you get them?" Izzy poked a hole in one of the blisters with her nail and popped out a tablet. It was bright yellow, stamped with a small circle. It smelled awful – like something rotten. She frowned at it, then glanced at the others. No one else seemed to be bothered.

"Internet. Obviously."

"The internet?"

"It's *fine*! I used the Maternal's account. She gets all her stuff from this pharmacy. Noxapharm or something."

"Well, that fills me with confidence..." Izzy couldn't tear her eyes away from the pill in her hand. Something about it felt ... off. Like that smell. Nothing good could smell like that, surely?

"Oh, come on. It's called 'Fokus*Pro*'. They wouldn't be allowed to call it that unless it had been tested and everything. It's literally just a bunch of algae and stuff. That's all it does. Helps you concentrate." Tigs scrunched up the paper bag and lobbed it across the room. "I mean, what's the worst that can happen, right?"

Chapter Two

As she glanced around the room, Izzy was relieved to see everyone looked as puzzled as she felt. Most of the others were doing exactly the same as she was – tipping the silver blister strips out of their packets and frowning.

"So. It goes like this." Tigs held up a hand to make sure they were all watching her. When Juliet was a fraction of a second too slow to look up, Tigs rolled her eyes and coughed. "Hello, Jools? This is kind of important."

"Sorry." Juliet looked like she wished the sofa would swallow her up.

"As I was saying…" Tigs leaned back against the glossy dark paintwork of the doorway, counting on her fingers. "Three strips of pills. Twelve pills in each strip. One pill every four hours you're studying, up to a maximum of four doses a day."

Noah narrowed his eyes, watching Tigs from the

end of the sofa. "So you're saying there's —" his eyes rolled towards the ceiling as he did the maths — "nine days' worth of this stuff?"

"I think that's what I just said, wasn't it?"

"Well, no. What you said was—"

"Fine." Tigs was already starting to look bored. "Four of these a day and then it's done. Exams will be a walk in the park and we can get on with the summer."

"You know there's more than nine days till the end of our exams, though, right?" Noah had folded his arms across his chest and was watching Tigs, one eyebrow raised.

She sighed. "Thank *God* you're here, Noah. I don't know how I'd have figured that out without you." As she spoke, she stepped away from the door and sidled up to him, patting him on the head. From the way he winced, Izzy thought she probably did it a little harder than she needed to. "Look, how you plan your revision timetable's totally up to you. I'm just the one saving your sad little futures right now, not your nanny."

Izzy still didn't like it. The whole idea of taking some kind of pill that Tigs (of all people) had ordered over the internet made her uneasy. What was in them, exactly? It was all very well saying it was vitamins and seaweed, but how could they know for sure? And that was before even considering the fact it was basically a study drug. Whatever Tigs said, it still felt like cheating, somehow.

Despite all this, Izzy couldn't quite bring herself to hand the pills back – not even to put them on the table in the middle of the room and leave them there.

After all, no one else was. And even though they were friends now, sitting in Tigs's ridiculous apartment at the top of a tower, in a couple of weeks they would be sitting at the narrow desks of the exam hall, and each one of them would be completely on their own. When it came to the results, there was only one top spot on the list – everyone else was just a high-ranking loser. It was the first thing anyone learned about life at Clerkenwell.

Izzy slid the blister strips back into the box and pushed it into the pocket of her jeans. She didn't have to take any of them, did she? But this way, at least she could make that choice later on, depending on how the revision was going.

It wasn't like they hadn't known the exams were coming. They'd been prepped and prepped and then prepped some more. There had been mock exams, and mocks for those, too. And now. Now it was the real thing. These exams wouldn't just grade them, individually and as a group. It also graded the school in the league tables, and nobody wanted to be the one to bring the average score down.

Izzy rubbed her hands together, trying to warm up her palms. The peculiar chill she'd felt earlier seemed to have sunk right into her bones and made them ache. Maybe it was all in her head – nobody else seemed to be bothered. It was just her imagination. She was worried, that was all. Worried that someone would talk – that one of the others might not be able to keep the secret. Worried about getting caught. And what would happen then? Did any of the others have as much to lose as she did?

The atmosphere in the room had relaxed, and Tigs had turned her attention to perching on the arm of the chair currently occupied by Grey, all the while flipping her glossy hair back over her shoulder. She was studiously ignoring him which – if Izzy knew Tigs, and she was pretty sure she did – meant that she was trying to work out a way of 'falling' off the chair and into his lap. When it came to Grey, Antigone Price was the embodiment of that old quote about never, ever, ever, *ever* giving up. Grey didn't get a say in the matter.

That was quite enough for Izzy. She walked over to the sliding glass door on to the balcony that ran the whole width of the flat, hauling it open and stepping out into the cool air. All of the City – and, beyond, all of London – lay spread out below her. It wasn't like the view from her own family's flat was bad, either, but the difference between the thirteenth floor and the thirty-fifth was staggering. From up here, people were no bigger than ants, tiny coloured specks bustling this way and that, threading through the Barbican's walkways to the complex at the centre, or heading back out towards the Tube. Izzy peered over the metal railing, holding on tight and pressing her knees against the glass panel below it.

"Long way down…" she whispered into the wind. That was the other thing about being this high up – it was never not windy. It could be the calmest summer day imaginable down at ground level, but this high up, there was never less than a stiff breeze.

It tugged at her hair, whipping it out over the rail. Izzy tried not to look down again, but she couldn't help it. It was the same every time she came up here, and the same every time she went out on her own balcony. Her eyes were always drawn downwards, as she imagined how long it would take to fall…

Forcing herself to let go of the rail, she took a step back into the safer territory of the balcony, towards the windows and the rough concrete wall. Her fingers ached as she uncurled them. She hadn't realized just how tightly she'd been gripping on. And that was since she'd got the better of her fear of heights. There hadn't been much choice, had there, after they'd moved into a tower block. However expensive or sought-after the flats might be, they were still a long way off the ground.

A quiet *swoosh* noise behind her, followed by a *click* startled Izzy and she turned round to see Tigs smiling at her from the other side of the sliding door.

Which was closed.

Tigs's fingers were resting on the locking mechanism.

"Tigs…" Izzy brushed her hair back from her face, but the wind blew it straight back again. "Tigs!"

There was a solid *clunk* as Tigs swung the locking handle into place. From the other side of the glass, she smiled sweetly at Izzy, and then lifted her other hand. She was holding a small remote control. Batting her eyelashes, she tipped her head to one side and pressed one of the buttons on the little remote. The curtains on the inside of the glass swished smoothly closed.

Izzy was shut out and cut off.

"Hey!" she shouted at Tigs, but there was no answer. Of course there wasn't. She was already homing in on Grey again and this was her way of making sure Izzy was out of the picture.

Not that there was a picture for her to be in, anyway. It didn't seem to matter how many times Izzy said it, Tigs never believed her. There wasn't anything between her and Grey. Never had been and sure as hell never would be. It was, funnily enough, one of the first conversations she and Tigs had ever had – if 'conversation' could also mean 'Tigs warning her that Grey was off-limits, whether he liked it or not'. It hadn't bothered Izzy at first. All she'd wanted was to fit in, to settle into her new school, new home, new life and to put the past behind her. She'd got it – Tigs was marking her territory, defending her pack, whatever. Now, though, it was getting annoying.

"Tigs!" Izzy banged her hand on the window. "Not funny!"

Again, there was no response.

"Well, that's just great," Izzy sighed and turned away from the window. There was nothing for it but to wait until Tigs decided to grow up and open the door. Might as well enjoy the view...

Lights were starting to come on in some of the windows in the long, low blocks that made up most of the rest of the Barbican. In other flats, the balcony doors were slid open as people came home from work and stepped out into the evening air. A gust of wind blew a snatch of music up, even to this height, from whatever was happening on the forecourt of the Barbican centre. It sounded like jazz, briefly, and then it was gone. On the far side of the complex, the glass office towers of the City were still buzzing with activity. Tiny little desks sat in rows along the glass sides, as if in a vast dolls' house.

And Izzy? Izzy was locked on a balcony.

There was a *clunk* from the far end of the balcony. Izzy looked round and straightened her hair – apparently Tigs had taken less time to get a grip than usual. But it wasn't Tigs who stuck her head round the door of one of the bedrooms. It was Kara. Izzy's hair whipped into her eyes yet again, and for a second she envied Kara's short hair. At least she didn't have to worry about the wind.

"I thought you'd been gone a while," Kara said.

"Yeah. She's got a weird sense of humour, hasn't she?" Izzy nodded to the locked door and the drawn curtains.

Kara smiled sadly. "Tell me about it. Tigs has always been like this. Don't take it personally. I spent the first couple of years I knew her thinking it was just a thing. Thinking she'd wake up one morning and we'd just be fine, you know?" She looked out over the City, then back to Izzy. "But this is just how she is. She doesn't like people getting too close."

"Like anyone gets the chance."

"Yeah, well. You better come back in before she realizes I've opened the door. She'll kill me." Kara was no longer smiling.

Great as the view might be, Izzy wasn't going to hang around on the balcony any longer, and she quickly followed Kara back inside They hurried through what was obviously a spare room – with a bed that Izzy guessed was as big as her entire bedroom, piled high with velvet and silk cushions – and slipped out into the long hallway. Laughter trickled down from the far end.

Izzy followed the sound to the kitchen, where she found Grey backed into a corner beside the enormous fridge. Between him and the door was, of course, Tigs. Making the most of her opportunity, she had switched into full-on flirt mode and was leaning in so close to him that Izzy was surprised she hadn't actually started trying to climb into his arms. Typical Grey, he looked completely unfazed by any of it, which must have been driving Tigs crazy. She used her charm like a weapon and, normally, it knocked people sideways – parents, teachers, half a dozen of the guys from school. And now Grey. Only nobody had ever told Grey that that was how it was supposed to go.

He caught sight of Izzy standing in the kitchen doorway and his face brightened.

"Where'd you go?" he said, more or less shoving Tigs out of the way as he tried to squeeze past her.

"Needed some air. Got a bit more than I was expecting." Izzy raised an eyebrow at Tigs, who pouted.

"God. Some people can't take a joke." There was a sour note in Tigs's voice, but it seemed like that was the end of it.

From the living room, there was the sound of someone clearing their throat. "So," said Mia. "Are we going to do some work or what?"

"You're actually kidding me?" said Tigs as she led the way out of the kitchen. "You want to work? Tonight?"

"Look, maybe your mum's not going to be quizzing you on how to work out the volume of a cone over breakfast…"

"Dude." Noah was looking through the huge collection of pristine books on the shelves across the room, the spines all arranged by colour. He didn't even look away from the bookcase. "It's one-third pi r-squared by height. You totally know that."

"That's not the point…" Mia was blushing.

Izzy dropped on to the sofa beside Mia and nudged her. "Don't mind Noah. It's not like he can *help* being a know-it-all."

Noah snorted. "Oh, sure I can. Maybe I just *like* being one." He grinned at Izzy, who threw a notebook at him, aiming directly for his head.

Noah ducked as it flew across the room. It clattered against the window and he straightened up again, glancing behind him. "Shame. Want to try again?"

"The point is—" Mia raised her voice slightly, trying to be heard over Noah.

"We get the point. You want to be dull and actually, like, revise. Well, *fine*." Tigs flung herself across a giant floor cushion. "You're no fun at all."

"I'm plenty of fun. I'll just be more fun once the exams are over." Mia started to flip through the pages of her folder.

"Hey, Tigs." Dom leaned towards the cushion from his spot on the floor. "You know who's *really* fun…?"

"Spare me. Just … no." Tigs held up her hand. Dom grinned, and Izzy tried not to smile. Of *course* Tigs would assume that he was seriously hitting on her.

"What do you want to start with? History or maths?" Mia spread a few sheets of paper across the table, pushing all the folders to one side. Everyone groaned.

"Can't we start with something easy? Like Mandarin?" Dom asked.

"Mandarin's only easy for *you* guys, remember?" Izzy laughed. She could see Dom wriggling his box of FokusPro out of his pocket, turning it over to open it. Mia glanced up, watching her brother thoughtfully, but said nothing.

"Yeah. And Noah." Dom tapped a strip of tablets out on to the table.

"Hey!" Noah was obviously starting to feel picked on. It didn't usually stop them. Dom teased him because Noah was his best friend, and Mia teased Noah because Dom was doing it. And Mia *always* had to do whatever her twin was doing, even if it didn't necessarily work the other way around.

"That's because Noah's a freak." Tigs said the last word a little too loudly, a little too brightly. Izzy didn't like the way it sounded – petty and unkind, and jealous. It wasn't exactly Noah's fault that he was smarter than the rest of them put together, was it? And it wasn't like he taunted them with it. Not the way Tigs liked to taunt them with her family's money, or her connections, or her home.

Maybe Antigone Price was the devil, but it was sure as hell better to have the devil on your side than not.

"Maths," said Mia. "Seeing as our resident swot has started us off; Noah, how do you calculate the volume of a frustum?"

"A what?" muttered Dom. He had already punched out one of the little yellow pills and was rolling it around in his hand thoughtfully.

"Keep up. A frustum. A cone with the pointy bit cut off?"

"How the hell d'you know that?"

"It's in the notes?" Mia held up her folder, turning the page to face her brother and displaying it to everyone. Sure enough, there was a neat drawing of a squat cone, and a column of equations and numbers.

"Huh," said Dom. "Better hope this works, then, hadn't I?" And without another word, he dropped the pill into his mouth and threw his head back to swallow it.

All around her, Izzy saw the others doing the same, pulling faces as the taste of the pills caught on their tongues. Grey winked at her as he swallowed his. "Down the hatch," he said, then coughed. "Wow. That is *foul*."

Izzy looked at the little yellow circle in her hand. She didn't really remember pulling the pack out of her pocket, or tipping the tablet on to her palm. But she obviously had, because there it was. Looking right back at her.

"You need a drink?" Noah was holding out a can of whatever sugar-loaded drink he happened to be favouring that month. It was bright orange, and however bad a taste the FokusPro might leave, Izzy suspected that might be worse. She shook her head, smiling. "No, thanks. I'm good."

And she dropped the tablet on to her tongue, tipping her head back and swallowing. The pill caught in her throat and for a second, she thought it was going to stick there forever. She swallowed again, hard, and thankfully this time it went down. When she looked up, everyone was staring at her.

Izzy coughed feebly, and banged a hand on her chest. "Got stuck," she muttered. It was good enough for everyone, it seemed, and they all turned their attention to the surface area of a cylinder. All except Kara, who was looking thoughtfully at the palm of her hand. Izzy watched from the corner of her eye as Kara very quietly tucked her small yellow pill down the side of the cushion.

Chapter Three

Izzy hadn't realized that time could go so fast. Every day of study leave was the same – she would get up and drag herself to the kitchen to find some breakfast and coffee, then drag herself back to her room, where she spent the entire morning with her head firmly stuck in her books. At some point in the morning, there would be a text from Grey, asking if she had the notes from yet another class he'd completely forgotten. They had it down to a fine art now. He'd text her, she'd dig out the notes and trudge to the front door, cross the hall and call the lift. When the doors opened, she dropped the notes on the floor inside and pressed the button for the eighteenth floor. Then she'd wait for the lift to come back down to the thirteenth with whatever notes he'd borrowed yesterday.

At some point, if she remembered, there would be a sandwich, and then it was back to work. The hours blurred, and more than once she had heard the front door open and her dad calling her name and been surprised that he was home so early, only to look at the clock and realize it was almost ten at night and he'd brought dinner back with him.

And so it went. Her eyes felt gritty and hot and she didn't think she'd slept for more than four or five hours a night since the last day of term. She had a headache that wouldn't shift no matter how many painkillers she threw at it. The inside of her head felt buzzy, as though a fine trickle of sand was constantly running down the inside of her skull. It was impossible to tell whether it was the stress and the pure panic of the looming exams getting ever closer, the lack of sleep or the sheer amount of information she was trying to cram into her brain. Dates of Richard II's reign? Got it. How a blast furnace works? No problem. Newton's four laws of… No, there were three, weren't there? Newton's *three* laws of motion. Had it down.

Izzy wondered whether anyone had ever experimented to see how much stuff a brain could hold before it exploded. And, if they had, would knowing the results make her feel better or worse?

So far, she'd done her best to ignore the quiet little voice at the back of her mind that kept saying could it possibly be the FokusPro making her feel so strange. Because the little voice was wrong, wasn't it?

It was true that the scratching feeling had started the morning after she'd taken that little yellow tablet. It was true that the cold sensation she'd had the first time she held the pills had now settled in the pit of her stomach and didn't ever quite seem to go. It was true that after a full day taking them her fingers tingled and the edges of her vision took on a strange, sparkly effect. And that was without even thinking about the dreams she'd been having.

Yes, all these things were true. *But.* Within half an hour of taking that first dose of FokusPro, Izzy had felt more awake than she ever had. More *focused.* Her class notes made sense. Even the funny little scribbly bits where she'd obviously been in a rush or hadn't got a clue what was going on and had just copied things off the whiteboard word for word. More importantly, she could remember it all. Everything she'd covered in these endless, endless revision sessions. Not just bits here and there. All of it. Every single word. She could not only picture the pages in her folders or textbooks, see the words arranged on the paper as clearly as if they were spread out in front of her – she could follow them exactly. She knew what they meant, she knew how to apply all the theories, how to make them *work*. It wasn't that the pills made her smarter – at least, she didn't think that was it. It was more like they helped her shut out everything except the notes.

Well. Everything except the notes and the scratching inside her head.

And dreams were only dreams. They weren't real. But exams were. Results were.

There had been the awkward moment one morning when, deep into the Peasants' Revolt, her dad had appeared in her bedroom doorway – yesterday's shirt unbuttoned at the neck and his tie scrunched in one hand. In the other, he held one of the blister strips of pills, waving it back and forth like a metronome.

"Do I need to be worried about this?" he'd asked, frowning at her.

Izzy shook her head. "They're just a study aid."

"Mmm-hmm." He looked sceptically at the packet in his hand. "And where did they come from?"

"Health food shop." The lie was surprisingly easy.

44

"Really?"

"The one down on Cheapside. You know?" Izzy flipped a page of her textbook.

"I see," he sighed. "You'd tell me, wouldn't you? If there was something…"

"Yes, Dad. I'd tell you."

"Promise?" He looked earnest.

"Yes, Dad. I promise." She tried to hide the smile that was threatening to creep across her face. It wasn't that he didn't trust her – she knew that. He just worried about her. More since her mum had left; since they'd moved to the Barbican. She tried to see it as his way of showing he cared. After all, her mother had left him, too.

He'd hovered a little longer in the doorway. "Just … don't get too caught up in all this, OK? They're only exams, you know. In a few years, no one's going to care what kind of results you get. The last thing I want is for you to push yourself too hard. Like you did at your other school…" He let the sentence hang in the air. Izzy tried to ignore it.

"A few years is still a few years away, though, isn't it?" She shrugged and nodded towards the tie in his hand. "Are you staying at home today?"

"No such luck, I'm afraid." He tossed the pill strip over to her. "Just came back to change my shirt." He plucked at the fabric of his white shirt between his finger and thumb. "Everyone's flat out on this project. I've just sent the team out to have a break and get some air."

"You were working all night? Again?" It wasn't much of a surprise to Izzy really. She'd got increasingly used to finding his bedroom untouched in the mornings, the bed unslept in.

"It won't be for much longer. We have a couple of days to get all the systems up and running, and then there's the presentation to the board in Frankfurt… And then life goes back to normal. I promise." He stepped into the room and dropped a kiss on the top of her head. "I'll take some leave over the summer. We'll go out and do things."

"Promise?"

"I promise." He smiled at her, even as he copied the same tired tone of voice she'd just used when she said the same thing to him. "Love you, sweetie."

"Love you, too, Dad."

"Good luck with the revision." He ducked back out of the room again and she was just about to ask him to stop – to tell him that she had lied about the pills, to tell him the truth – when she heard his bedroom door close.

It wasn't worth it. It would all be over soon and then the summer stretched out ahead of them. A summer that was mostly going to be spent lying on the grass in the Barbican gardens. Kara had a summer job lined up in the Barbican theatre, but it wasn't like she needed the money, was it? She was so crazy about the theatre that she'd probably have paid *them* to let her work there.

That was all very well, but there was no way that Izzy was going to be doing anything other than enjoying the rewards of having worked so stupidly hard for the exams.

The Clerkenwell School had its own dedicated exam hall. Some schools just used a couple of classrooms with the desks rearranged into long, straight lines. Or maybe they used the gym. The assembly hall. Something like that. Clerkenwell wasn't like other schools, and so it had its own full-time exam space. When it wasn't being used for real exams like these, it was used for mocks – just so nobody ever forgot that Clerkenwell was All About Results. Three times a year, without fail, every single student sat down to a series of exams on every subject they took. And three times a year, without fail, a handful of pupils left the school after their last paper of the session and didn't come back.

No pressure or anything.

Ahead of the day's first exam, they all lined up against the wall, waiting for the doors to open, like cows outside a slaughterhouse. If, that is, cows had bundles of revision notes on little cue-cards that they were frowning over in the hope of cramming something at the last minute, or if cows had spent an entire afternoon traipsing round the City of London trying to find a stationery shop that sold clear plastic pencil cases. Tigs had, naturally, decided the rules about what you could take into the exam hall didn't apply to her and instantly vowed to take revenge on the invigilator who confiscated her Louis Vuitton pencil case. Izzy had to choke back a laugh at her wail of, "But it's monogrammed!" echoing around the exam hall.

It didn't take long to get back into the routine they all knew. They were herded in, they found their assigned desks and they sat down. They wrote for an hour and a half, they got up and they left. Some days, they did it all over again straight after lunch. Twice.

After a day or two, Izzy thought as she traipsed out of yet another session (Science II) rubbing her aching wrist, it felt like the most natural thing in the world. Provided you could ignore the inevitable cry of "I am not a number!" from Grey every time they were told to write their candidate numbers clearly in the space on the front page of their papers.

Izzy studied, she turned up on time, she gave up anything resembling a social life and she crossed off the exams marked on the calendar with thick black permanent marker.

The only hint of drama came later, midway through the second history paper. It had all been going fine – the sun was shining, the clock was ticking quietly and they had been blessed with an invigilator who was much happier sitting on a chair at the front of the room than constantly walking up and down the aisles between the desks with squeaky shoes or soles that clacked with every … single … step. As far as Izzy was concerned, it was an easy paper. She knew this stuff, after all, and although she didn't have quite the same kind of tunnel-vision focus that she'd had while she had been revising and taking the FokusPro, the after-effects of the pills were only just fading. Reluctant as she was to give Tigs any kind of credit, it looked like she'd been right. The FokusPro was *just* what they'd needed. Just what *she'd* needed.

So it was quiet, and everyone was writing, and there were only four papers left to sit before everyone was free to spend the summer doing whatever they wanted. And then, midway through the session, there came the unmistakable sound of someone in the room starting to cry.

It was muffled at first, as though whoever it was had hidden their face behind a sleeve in an effort to keep quiet. But then it grew louder and louder, less controlled, until it wasn't so much a sniffle as full-on weeping. People looked up from their desks. Dom, sitting in front of Izzy, turned round in his seat and mouthed, "Who is it?" She shrugged, but all the same, she twisted round in her chair and tried to work out who'd been broken by Clerkenwell this time. The weeping built to a wail, and then to a howl. It was coming from the back of the hall, and everyone had stopped writing. People were craning their necks, leaning out to the side to see who it was.

The invigilator looked up from his book and sighed. "Is there a problem?" he asked, his voice a little louder than it needed to be. Nobody paid any attention.

"I said, is there a problem?" He dropped his book on the floor. Everyone ignored him. Despite the strict no-talking rule in the exam room, people were starting to whisper to one another.

"Quiet down, now. Is—" Whatever the question was, nobody got to hear the end of it. There was another howl from the rear of the hall, and the sound of a chair scraping back across the parquet floor and someone trying to get out from behind their desk. A faint scuffling, and then the almighty clatter of the desk turning over and hitting the floor.

Izzy watched as Kara fled the exam room in floods of tears.

"So, what was with Kara's total meltdown?" Tigs held out her empty cup, swinging her feet back and forth as she sat on the low wall. Juliet shrugged and poured from the plastic jug of punch she was holding, then pushed her glasses back up her nose. It felt safe to talk about it now. The exams had finished that morning, with another science paper that could only be described as 'brutal' (or by Tigs as, "the worst thing that has ever, ever happened to me. Ever."). No one had wanted to bring up the subject of Kara's freak-out before all the papers were done. It had felt like bad luck, somehow. Like jinxing them when they were doing so well.

"Has anyone even seen her since?" Tigs continued when Juliet had topped up her drink.

"I've tried calling her," Juliet sighed. "Her phone's going straight to voicemail and she's not replied to any of my texts. I was hoping she'd come tonight."

"Did you go round to her place?" Izzy asked.

"I went round this afternoon but there was no one at home."

"Well, she didn't turn up for any of the maths papers. Maybe she's sick?" Izzy fished a bit of mint out of her drink. It stuck to her fingers no matter how hard she tried to shake it off, so eventually she gave up and ate it. Music spilled through the open door behind them, and candles flickered in old jam jars on the ground or hanging from the nearest branches, while fairy lights twinkled in the surrounding bushes.

They were in the garden outside Juliet's place, and it was Juliet's birthday. The lower floor of all the townhouse-style apartments on this side of the Barbican opened straight out on to the large residents' garden – each had their own small square of paving, and then the whole of the shared garden spread out in front of them. Tigs might have the best view, but Juliet had the grass. There were rules about using the garden at night – almost all of which came down to the fact that no one was supposed to. Most of the group were lounging under the spreading walnut tree that shaded the path around the edge of the lawn. Juliet went inside to fetch another jug of revoltingly sweet fruit punch from the kitchen. And, feeling bad that it was Juliet's birthday party and everyone seemed to be treating her like some kind of waitress, Izzy went to help. When they emerged from the kitchen, Dom leaped to his feet.

"Sweet sixteen, baby!" he whooped at Juliet as he stumbled through the branches and ducked inside. He was doing a lot of that – making excuses to go in and out, passing them at every opportunity. And every time he did, he said something to Juliet. And every time he did *that*, she turned bright red beneath her glasses and fiddled with the edge of the dress she'd bought specially. Not to impress Dom, of course – despite the fact that it was dark green, his favourite colour, and printed all over with tiny red roses.

"Uh-huh…" said Izzy, nudging her.

"Shut up," Juliet mumbled into her hair. She turned an even deeper shade of red.

Tigs looked from Izzy to Juliet, and then turned to watch Dom's back disappear into the kitchen. "Really? *Dom?*"

"What?" Juliet's voice changed at the merest hint of disapproval from Tigs. "What's wrong with Dom?"

"Oh. Nothing. I mean, he's not my type but if *you* like him…"

Izzy sighed. Typical Tigs – to take something Juliet was excited about and squash it like a bug. "Shut *up*, Tigs."

The evil look Tigs shot her didn't go unnoticed, either, but Izzy turned back towards Juliet and took the jug of punch out of her hands.

"I say go for it," she said with a grin. "Don't listen

to her! Go enjoy your birthday or something." Izzy gave Juliet a gentle shove towards the others. She watched Juliet flop down on to the grass beside Mia, smiling and smoothing out the skirt of her new dress.

"You know, you can be a real bitch, Tigs."

"What? Just because I'm not sucking up to Juliet?"

"Seriously. Shut up. This whole 'mean girl' act gets a bit old sometimes."

"Who says it's an act?" Tigs shot back.

"Uh-huh. Right."

"Why d'you care what she thinks, anyway? Look at her – she doesn't care what *we* think, does she?" Tigs nodded towards Juliet, who was sitting under the tree opening a birthday card. The shadows cast by the fairy lights and the flickering candles danced across the ground behind her. For a second, they almost looked like fingers reaching out for her, stretching out across the grass and up her back, catching in her hair.

And then Izzy leaned forward to dodge the party poppers that Noah had let off over her head and the illusion was broken.

Dom stuck his head back out through the door. "D'you think it's dark enough yet?" he asked, peering up at the evening sky. Izzy followed his gaze. From the gardens, even the lowest blocks of the Barbican loomed six storeys overhead. Directly behind them, Lauderdale Tower – where Izzy and Grey lived – looked like it was tall enough to pierce the clouds. (Although Tigs would always be quick to point out that Shakespeare Tower was, in fact, *taller* and therefore obviously *better.*) Even though it was June, and the day had been hot and sunny, there wasn't a whole lot of evening sunlight to be found in the gardens and at ground level, dusk was gathering fast. Across the gardens, the lights on the front of the Barbican Centre itself glowed through the trees.

"Dark enough for what? You'll have to wait ages if you want it to get properly dark. Best you're going to get for a while is slight gloom." Izzy realized she was talking to an empty doorway, so stepped inside to see exactly what he was up to.

"Can't have a birthday party without a cake, can you?" Dom was rummaging around in a supermarket carrier bag. Eventually, he found what he was looking for – a packet of pink candles – and stuck them all over the top of the cake he'd unpacked.

"Pink?" Izzy flicked one of the candles with her fingernail.

"She's a girl, isn't she?"

"Not all girls love pink, you know."

"Oh…"

"I'm kidding. It's fine – she'll love it."

"So, Juliet *does* like pink?"

"You got her a birthday cake and candles, Dom. I don't think she's going to care what colour they are." She watched his face light up. So maybe there was something there after all. "You should ask her out."

"What? No. I… I couldn't…" He was suddenly deeply interested in lighting the candles.

"Why not?"

"What if she said no?"

"Trust me, Dom." Izzy patted him on the shoulder and held the door to the garden open for him. She could see Juliet looking around for someone and Izzy didn't think for one second that Juliet was looking for *her.* "She's not going to say no."

As he stepped past her, carefully carrying the cake in front of him, Dom's face glowed red in the candlelight. A chorus of voices (some less in tune than others) started to sing 'Happy Birthday' and Juliet clamped her hands over her mouth in happy surprise.

The cake, as it turned out, was so good that even Tigs couldn't resist it. "It's fine," she said as she licked chocolate icing off her fork. "I found some of Mother's diet supplements in the cupboard. They just burn the fat off you."

"You ever look what's in those things?" Grey asked, leaning back on his elbows and staring up at the branches overhead.

Tigs shrugged. "Like I said before – if they weren't safe, they wouldn't be allowed to sell them."

"But they're not, are they? You can't exactly get all this stuff in Boots, can you? You're buying it from some dodgy place on the internet."

"I didn't see you complaining when I came up with the FokusPro," Tigs sniffed back at him. "You all took it, didn't you?"

No one answered.

"Well. Everyone except Kara," said Mia quietly. As one, they all looked at her. "What?" Mia sounded defensive. "She said she didn't like the idea. That it felt like cheating."

"So she didn't take any of them?" Noah blinked

at Mia as though he couldn't quite believe what he was hearing. Even Noah, their very own genius, had struggled enough with the pressure and the sheer amount of revision that he'd taken the pills. And if *he'd* needed them…

"I guess that explains her little outburst in the exam hall, then, doesn't it?" said Tigs. She was still licking her fork, even though it was by this point the cleanest fork in the history of all forks. "She just couldn't hack it."

"And nobody's seen her since? Don't you think we should check up on her?" Izzy shifted uncomfortably. The grass was starting to feel damp. Clammy. The sky had darkened another shade, and now the shadows around the edges of the garden were thicker and heavier than they had been earlier.

Izzy had never really been in the gardens when they were empty – it had always been daytime, and there was always someone around. It wasn't crowded, true, but there was still a feeling that you weren't really alone in the middle of the Barbican. Now, however, the gardens felt deserted – even knowing that there were people on the lakeside terrace, getting drinks or having a meal. Even knowing there were faces behind so many of the windows that overlooked the gardens, passers-by on the walkways above, somehow, the place felt hostile, as though they were intruders.

Maybe it was because Izzy knew she'd felt exactly the same as Kara when Tigs handed out those packets of pills. That it felt like cheating. And she'd still taken them, anyway. Kara hadn't. Kara had done what she thought was the right thing – what even *Izzy* thought was the right thing – and look where it had got her.

The others felt the change, too. She could tell. Everyone was suddenly a little less relaxed, a little less comfortable. A breeze shivered the branches above them and made the lights flicker and the jam jars rattle against each other. Juliet looked up at them nervously. "We should probably head inside. I don't want any of the busybody neighbours complaining…"

"Wait." Dom was standing with his back to them all, looking out into the garden.

"Dom…" Izzy started, meaning to tell him that now really wasn't the time to ask Juliet out. But then he made a hissing sound.

He was looking at something.

"Did you see that?" he asked, not moving. Whatever it was, his eyes were fixed on it.

"See what?" Grey ducked past Izzy and stood shoulder to shoulder with Dom, peering into the shadows.

"Over there…" Dom nodded towards the bushes at the far side of the grass. They were tucked into a corner, where the side of one of the low blocks met the edge of the girls' school that sat next to the lake. In the fading light, it was almost impossible to work out where the bushes ended and the wall began, but still Dom was staring at them.

"I think there's something … some*one* in there. Watching us."

Chapter Four

"What did you say?" Izzy was sure she must have misheard. "Because it sounded like…"

"There's someone in there, watching us. I'm sure." Dom was completely focused on the bushes.

"It's probably just a cat," Izzy said, peering at the plants.

"In the Barbican? Not likely," Grey snorted.

"Fine. A fox, then," Izzy laughed.

But Dom really meant it. "I'm telling you…" he said, and he took a step forward, but Grey suddenly put out his arm and stopped him.

"No. You stay here. I'll go – it's probably nothing, all right?"

Instinctively, the rest of the group had drawn into a huddle. The flickering candles in the jam jars no longer looked magical. Now they looked like warning lights, like alarms. Izzy stopped right where she was, midway between Dom and the others. Grey was already strolling, as casually as he could, over the lawn towards the darkened corner.

It was unsettling, the idea that someone might be watching them. What, exactly, were they hoping to see? And why were they hiding? It was more than unsettling. It was *creepy*.

Grey carried on walking towards the bushes. It was already harder to pick him out against the shadows. Dom was still watching, eagle-eyed.

"What's going on?" Juliet's voice sounded stretched. Strained. All the joy had been sucked clean out of it.

"It's…" Izzy turned to face the others, and froze. Behind them, lights blazed in the windows of Juliet's home; the kitchen door stood open. And someone ran across the doorway.

"Juliet…"

"What?"

"Are your parents working tonight?"

"Yes. Why?"

"I think there's somebody in your house."

It had moved too fast for Izzy to make it out clearly, but it had definitely been a figure disappearing behind the doorframe.

"There's nobody over here," Grey called from across the lawn. He was already starting to jog back.

Noah made a *stay put* gesture to Juliet. "I'll go check the house."

"You can't go on your own!" Juliet called after him. She was right – they'd all seen enough films to know that nothing good ever happened to anyone who went off on their own to check an empty house.

"I'll go with him," Izzy found herself saying, not entirely willingly. But she was sure she had seen something, whatever it was, and she couldn't just stand there while Noah walked into the house alone. "We'll go. Call the police, OK?"

"No." Juliet shook her head firmly. "My parents will kill me. I'm not supposed to be having a party."

"There's someone in your house and you're worried about your *parents* killing you?" Izzy fumbled in her pocket for her phone. As the screen lit up, she saw the depressingly familiar 'No signal' icon. "Oh, come on." She glanced up at the solid concrete hulks around them, silhouetted against the slowly darkening sky and dotted with lit windows. Being in the middle of a basin made of reinforced concrete never made for great phone reception – why would it be any different now? "Someone with a signal call the police. I'm not kidding..." she added, looking at Juliet's ashen face and hurrying after Noah towards the open door.

The white voile curtain that covered the door when it was closed, giving some privacy from the garden, fluttered around the doorway. The townhouse was bright and, at first glance, at least, welcoming. In the kitchen, the glossy red worktops reflected the spotlights set into the ceiling while beyond, the main hall was lit by a tall lamp designed to look like a light from a film set. Everything was absolutely still and silent until, just ahead of her, Noah stepped through the door and put one foot on the kitchen floor. The wood creaked loudly as he put first one foot and then another on the polished surface. She froze, holding her breath. Just listening.

Nothing.

Noah crept forward.

Izzy could feel her heart pounding against her ribs. What if there *was* someone here? What did they want? Or what if she was wrong, and it really all had been just a trick of the light? She glanced back to see the others, still standing together under the tree where Grey looked puzzled, almost nervous.

Something brushed against her neck…

She didn't even realize she was screaming until Noah grabbed her shoulders and shook her. "Izzy! Izzy! Get a grip!"

"I… What?" Noah hadn't been there a second ago – he'd been on the other side of the kitchen, hadn't he?

"What's wrong?"

"Nothing. There was somebody … something. Touching me."

"You mean like this?" He reached behind her and pushed the curtain back along its rail. It had shifted in the breeze and rubbed against the side of her neck. "Jesus, you almost gave me a heart attack, screaming like that. I was in the hall…"

"You were in the hall? And now you're here?"

"I was right by the stairs and then you started freaking out. Scared the hell out of me. And them." He nodded over her shoulder. Behind her, all the others were peering in through the door.

Grey stood a few steps further back from them, still outside and talking on his phone, shaking his head. "No. Sorry, Officer. I think it might be a false alarm. No, no need. There's no one here. We're fine. Yep.

Absolutely. Yep. Thanks." He hung up and looked back at Izzy, tipping his head on one side. "So the local plods think that we're either rich kids pranking them and wasting their time, or we just tried to murder you. Neither's going to make them like us, is it?"

"I don't get it." Izzy felt woozy all of a sudden. The ground seemed to tip sideways beneath her, and she found herself leaning on the worktop. "I was there, and Noah was over there ... and now you're all ... here..." She tailed off. It sounded stupid, even in her own head, but it was like she'd been watching a film that was missing a few frames and had suddenly skipped ahead. There wasn't much of a jump, but she was certain she'd missed *something*.

Noah narrowed his eyes at her. "You sure you're OK?"

"I don't know." Her heart was still pounding, and her head felt too heavy and too light at the same time. "Did you find anything? Is there...?"

"There's nobody here, Iz. No one. It's all fine."

"But I saw..."

Noah slid up on to the worktop, his legs dangling. "I don't think it was anything. It was just like when

Dom thought he saw something outside. Probably just the stupid candles. Weird lights, you know?"

"Weird lights?" Even when she was shaken up, Izzy knew when she was being patronized.

"I could give you the science thing, but … well." Noah shook his head theatrically and winked at her.

"Fine. Weird lights." She ran her hands back through her hair. It felt damp, sticky between her fingers. "I think I'm going to go home. Sorry, Juliet."

"What for?" Juliet was standing right next to Dom. *Right* next to him. He practically had his arm around her.

"Hope I didn't mess up your birthday? You know, with the seeing crazy stuff and the screaming?"

"It's been an awesome birthday. The best." She appeared to be blushing. And she was grinning from ear to ear – so, imaginary psycho or not, she'd obviously got exactly what she wanted for her birthday.

Grey edged into the kitchen past Noah's swinging legs. "I'll walk you back."

"Shut up. It's about thirty seconds to our lobby from here."

"Sure. Like the thirty seconds back then when you just went catatonic and started screaming."

"Point taken."

"Thought so. Come on." He held the door open. "Later," he said, to all of them and none of them in particular. There was a murmur of goodbye.

Izzy could barely speak, she felt so embarrassed. What was the *matter* with her? First of all she'd flipped out over seeing the shadow of a tree branch, and then she'd started screaming because a curtain touched her neck. Not good. Not good at all. She wanted to blame Dom – after all, he'd started it. Hadn't he been the one who'd seen someone hiding in the shadows? And hadn't he set them all on edge? But she didn't think she could. Not really. She'd felt off for a couple of weeks, now she thought about it. It was the exams, the revision, just the plain old pressure. All of it. The inside of her head still felt scratchy. Her skin felt too tight, like it had shrunk in the wash. No wonder she'd freaked out at the first sign of nothing.

Still, she thought as they reached the bottom of the steps up from the garden, it was summer now. The exams were behind them and they were totally free. Everything would settle down soon enough.

Grey unlocked the gate that closed off the bottom of the stairway and walked through it, holding it for her. She stepped through after him, and the gate closed behind them with a solid-sounding *clang*.

She felt better after a shower. Steam billowed out of the bathroom door as, wrapped in an enormous fluffy towel, she padded barefoot down the hallway to the kitchen. Izzy switched on the coffee machine and leaned across the kitchen counter to jab at the answerphone, its little display flashing with a bright red 'one'. The message was from her dad, of course.

Working late, don't wait up, don't worry. Sure. Always the same thing. She jabbed at the machine again, erasing his voice, and crossed to the balcony door. It slid open easily and she stepped out, the rough concrete of the balcony cold under her feet. Leaning over the rail, she could see his office building from where she stood. All glass and steel, the bank's flagship building glittered with light.

"Night, Dad." Izzy drummed her fingers on the rail.

Inside, the coffee machine gurgled and, a little

reluctantly, Izzy turned back to the kitchen – just in time to see the shadow pass the door at the end of the hall.

Suddenly, she didn't feel so warm any more. Or as good as she had a moment before.

She closed the door behind her as she stepped back inside, drawing her towel more closely around her. "Hello?"

There was no answer.

"Dad?"

Still nothing.

Of course it wasn't her dad. Hadn't she just listened to him saying he'd be home late?

"Hello?" She took a step to her right, out of the kitchen and into the hallway that ran the length of the apartment. She could see her footprints on the wooden floor – small puddles in the shape of her feet from the bathroom down to the kitchen door. Other than that, the hallway looked like it should. Like it always did. Empty.

"'Weird lights'. Yeah, right," she said. But as she turned back towards the kitchen, out of the corner of her eye she saw the door to her dad's bedroom at the end of the hall swing open a little.

"Dad? Are you home?" Even as she took a step down the hallway towards the open door, she knew it was a pointless thing to say because if he answered, either way, he was home. And if he didn't, then he wasn't. Or something like that.

There was no answer from behind the door.

"Dad?"

She was almost at the door, reaching a hand out for it.

Above her, the lights started to flicker.

"Dad? Is that you?"

Her heart was pounding so hard that she could feel it in her throat as her fingers pressed against the wood of the door, pushing it all the way open. In the hallway, the lights were flickering wildly, casting distorted shadows of her hand, twisting it into claws gouging into the wood.

The door swung open with a creak.

Nothing.

There was nobody there. The room was empty – the bed as neatly made as always, the chair in front of the window perfectly straight. The door on to the balcony was ajar, and a breeze ruffled the curtains.

In the hallway, the lights shone as brightly and steadily as ever, reflecting in her rapidly drying footprints.

Alone in the middle of the room, Izzy blew out a long, relieved breath and brushed her hair back from her face. "I have *got* to get some more sleep."

It was the pressure. Of course it was. The pressure of the exams, of keeping up with classwork and revision exercises. Of keeping up with everyone else, even out of school. The pressure of just being Izzy – good student, good friend, good person ... all of that. But it was all she had. She was never going to be an Antigone Price. It looked like everything just came so easily to Tigs. But then, wasn't that what she was used to? It was the thing that still kept Izzy in awe of her – she just *expected* things ... and then she got them. Designer handbag? Got one. Every gadget known to mankind? Yep. Guaranteed success in the exams, and a ticket to the best future money could buy? Well, maybe she needed a little help with that, but somehow she was still making it happen, wasn't she?

Izzy, on the other hand? Not quite the same deal. But it was fine, she thought, padding back down the hall to the kitchen. After all, would she really want to be Tigs? The image of her balancing on the arm of the chair, desperately trying to attract Grey's attention, flickered through Izzy's mind. No. When it really came down to it, she wouldn't.

In the kitchen, she picked a clean mug off the counter and reached for the coffee machine and then paused, her hand halfway there. "You know what? Maybe not," she said to nobody in particular, and instead, she flicked on the kettle and dropped a bag of jasmine tea into the bottom of her mug, shaking her head as she emptied the whole jug of freshly brewed coffee straight into the sink. "No more caffeine for you, Izzy. Not tonight. Or, you know, *ever* again."

As she carried her mug back up the hallway to her bedroom, she looked straight ahead, forcing herself to ignore the shadow that flashed along the balcony. She was tired. And, after all, it was just another trick of the light.

Chapter Five

Izzy's grandmother had always said that everything looks better after a good night's sleep, which had struck Izzy as fairly ironic, given that Grandma Whedon actually *died* in her sleep. But despite the bright sunshine and the blue sky, there seemed to be a quiet grey fog following Izzy around this morning. It had been there since the night of Juliet's party, two days ago. She'd put it down to post-exam jitters to begin with; to the release of all the stress. She'd had a quiet couple of days – reading, watching endless television and not doing a lot else.

She had hardly even seen her dad – his work project had more or less taken over his life. His big department presentation was coming up soon, and he'd barely been home long enough to change, never mind pack a bag for the trip. If he was around for more than a couple of minutes at the start or the end of the day she was lucky – or unlucky, seeing as he crashed through the apartment like a tornado, knocking stuff over and scattering ties and paperwork in his wake. Mentally picturing herself buried under a paperslide long before the cleaner came round, Izzy gathered up all the folders and reports and whatever-else, and dumped them on the desk in his study, then closed the door on the whole lot. She'd had quite enough of seeing piles of notes scattered about the place – even a ringbinder was enough to give her revision flashbacks.

Perhaps, she thought, as she poured granola in the vague direction of her bowl and spilled a good portion of it, the key bit of Grandma Whedon's philosophy was that it needed to be a *good* night's sleep, with the emphasis on 'good'. Picking up cereal clusters and raisins and tossing them back into her bowl, Izzy yawned. When was the last time she'd woken up feeling like she had actually had a good night's sleep, anyway? It hadn't been last night, that was for sure. She tossed a raisin up in the air, trying to catch it in her mouth. It missed. No, last night's sleep had – like the night before, and the night before that as far as she could remember – been rubbish. A restless sleep punctuated by dark, unpleasant dreams that left her feeling unsettled and even more tired than she had been when she'd closed her eyes.

It wasn't even as if she could remember what the dreams were about, either. It was just that she knew they'd been bad. Sliding on to the seat at the breakfast bar, she poked at her cereal with her spoon. There had been ... running. She'd been scared, she remembered that much. There had been broken glass that crunched under her feet, and a shadow that followed her wherever she went. There had been the sound of something soft hitting something solid, over and over again. There had been a scream – just one, sharp and short.

It was all uncomfortably familiar, like déjà vu. But they were only dreams.

The sudden thought of the shadowy figure she'd seen – or thought she'd seen – in Juliet's house made her shiver. That had *not* been a dream – that had been real enough, whatever the others said.

Maybe that would explain last night's dreams, and why she was sleeping so badly. And before then? It didn't take a genius (or Noah) to figure out that the exams had taken their toll. Mrs Alderman might have meant her comment about 'taking things seriously' as gentle encouragement, but for days all Izzy had heard in her head was, "They're going to kick you out."

She chewed her granola thoughtfully. She still remembered that first trip to Clerkenwell. The interview with the head who'd looked over her school reports and frowned, even when her dad had explained everything in excruciating detail. She had hoped they might cut her a little slack once they heard how her mother had decided that she'd rather take that job in Hong Kong than stay with her family after all... But no. That was not The Clerkenwell Way. At Clerkenwell, it didn't matter whether your dog was run over, your father died, your house flooded or you caught Ebola. Or all of the above. You still turned in your work on time and it had better be worth at least an A minus. And *that* was making allowances.

Shaking her head, she slipped her empty breakfast bowl into the sink. She scooped her keys off the worktop and checked her phone. There were five texts from Tigs, each sent a minute apart. All of them said exactly the same thing: *Waiting. Where are you?* They were supposed to meet downstairs at 10:30am, and Izzy was precisely one minute late. Which meant that Tigs had started to get impatient a good four minutes early.

Naturally, that couldn't be *her* fault...

The original plan had been to go to one of the big department stores at the far end of Oxford Street. Juliet had her birthday money to spend, and Tigs was "feeling the need for a new bag" – a need she felt several times a year. Juliet suggested Selfridges; Tigs snorted and said, "Selfridges is dead to me. *Dead.*" So Selfridges was out.

The new plan saw them getting on the Tube to Bond Street station so they could carry on arguing somewhere closer to the shops, at least.

Kara trailed quietly behind. It had been a surprise to see her standing with the others, especially after her vanishing act, but she met Izzy's gaze and shrugged as though she'd read her mind.

"What can I say? I might as well enjoy the summer, right?"

"Are you OK?"

"Not really. I mean ... I messed up, didn't I?"

"Maybe it's not so bad. There's always resits, right?" Izzy tried to sound upbeat.

"Yeah. Resits. You ever heard of those at Clerkenwell?" Although she was smiling, Kara's voice was flat.

"They'll understand." Izzy knew that was unlikely but she couldn't think what else to say.

"Maybe." Kara didn't sound like she believed it either. Instead, she smoothed her hand over her hair – cropped shorter than ever now school had finished. "Can we just … not talk about it?"

"Sure. Whatever you want." Izzy felt sorry for Kara, but a tiny part of her wondered whether Kara deserved it. After all, she'd been offered the pills, just like the rest of them. She just hadn't wanted it badly enough, had she? Izzy pushed the thought aside.

"Aren't we waiting for Mia?" she called to the others, who were already heading down the steps into Barbican Tube station.

Juliet shook her head. "She's not coming. Something about Dom…?"

"Since when has Mia wanted to stay in with her brother more than come shopping?"

"Maybe they've got some kind of thing going on.

Who can tidy their room the fastest, or who can work out the square root of a million and forty-three point whatever quickest. You know what they're like… Hey! That's my lipstick!" Juliet suddenly yelped at Tigs, who had opened her bag to get her Oyster card.

"It's so not," Tigs said dismissively.

"It is! I've been looking for that for *ages!*"

Tigs and Juliet swept through the ticket barriers, dressed in their matching skinny jeans and vintage band T-shirts – and still bickering. Kara followed and Izzy was just about to follow, too, when a wave of dizziness threatened to knock her sideways. Still clutching her Oyster card, she swayed as the station spun around her.

The others showed no sign of noticing and carried on towards the stairs down to the trains. They'd realize sooner or later.

Probably.

Still reeling, Izzy stepped back from the ticket barrier and leaned against the tiled wall.

Just breathe, she told herself. *In and out. In and out. You're just tired…*

She *was*. She was tired. But even that wasn't quite enough to explain the advert on the wall across from her.

Izzy had passed that poster every time she'd been through the station in the last few months. She'd lost count of the number of times she'd seen it – so many that she didn't really even see it any more. It was just there.

Now, however, she was looking at it. Really looking at it.

It was wrong.

It should have been a picture of a group of people on a train. Smiling, having a cup of coffee, reading a book, pointing at the scenery.

It still kind of was. There were still people sitting on a train, smiling, laughing, having a cup of coffee … but their faces had changed. They were more pointed – sharper. Their *teeth* were sharper. There were dark hollows under their eyes … eyes which suddenly seemed to be looking right *at* her.

"Get a grip, Iz. Just tired, just tired, get a grip…" she muttered to herself.

And then one of the people blinked.

"Izzy? Are you coming?" Juliet was leaning

back over the barrier, calling to her. Tigs and Kara stood a few steps behind. Tigs was playing with her phone.

"I'm…" Izzy closed her eyes, took a deep breath. She was fine.

She opened her eyes; looked at the poster.

It had changed again.

The people had all moved. Now, they were in a line, as though they were pressed against a window and looking out on to the ticket hall. Looking out at her.

Their faces twisted into grotesque smiles and then began to melt.

"I… I…" Izzy gulped helplessly at the air, at the poster, at the ticket hall. At everyone.

"You all right, love?" One of the station staff leaned out of the ticket window – and to Izzy's horror, his face began to twist and melt, too, his eyes sinking into deep hollows.

Horrified, she tore her gaze away from him, not able to do anything more than whimper, and looked towards Juliet. Only to see the same twisted grin on her face, too.

"Seriously. What the hell is wrong with you?"

Tigs was unhappy about the change of plan. It showed.

Most of what happened after the others had come back for her was a blur. Someone had sat her down – one of the ticket staff, she assumed – and opened the barrier for the others to come back through. Izzy remembered Juliet crouching in front of her, talking. At least, her mouth was moving but Izzy couldn't hear anything beyond a faint ringing in her ears.

Her friends had got her back home, somehow, and had sat her down on the sofa and were now looking concerned. Or at least Juliet and Kara were. Tigs was mostly looking pissed-off.

"I'm going to get you something to drink," said Kara.

"A green tea would be good," said Izzy. "Thanks."

Kara disappeared into the kitchen. There was a clatter of cupboard doors opening and closing, and the sound of the kettle being switched on.

Izzy shook her head. "I don't know what happened. It was just … the poster. The faces…" She tailed off. Neither of them got it.

"Faces?" Tigs crossed her arms.

"I can't explain it."

"Try. Because this little therapy session is not the way my day's supposed to be going."

"I'm tired, I guess." Izzy rubbed her eyes. "Not sleeping."

"You, too?" Juliet asked. They both looked at her. "I thought maybe it was just me. The exams and that. I feel like I've not slept for weeks."

"Me, too – exactly the same!" said Izzy.

"And if I actually do get to sleep, it doesn't seem to matter how long it's for, I don't feel any better."

"Yes!" Izzy nodded at Juliet. So she wasn't the only one...

"God. Why don't you just take a sleeping pill if you're having that much trouble?" Tigs shook her head as though she couldn't believe what she was hearing. "It's what they're for."

"Not all of us have a chemist's shop in our bathroom cupboard, Tigs. And besides, those things are bad for you – you're not supposed to take them unless you have to."

"And I do. Like when I need my beauty sleep." Tigs smiled sweetly. "You two could do with some of that."

"Back off, Tigs. I'm not in the mood," Izzy snapped.

Tigs frowned. "Wow. Seriously – I'll give you some of the Maternal's sleeping pills. Your need is clearly greater…"

"I don't want any more pills, Tigs! Would you just leave it?" Izzy ran her hands through her hair, pulling it back. Her heart was pounding hard against her ribs again. She could feel her pulse beating in her neck.

"All right!" Tigs held up her hands and took a step back. "No need to be so psychotic about it."

"I'm not. I just… What?" Izzy stopped.

"I don't like being shouted at."

"I wasn't!"

"Uh…" Juliet cut in, "sorry, Izzy, but you were."

"Oh."

She hadn't been shouting, had she? She didn't think she had. She certainly hadn't meant to… But the two of them were standing over her and looking like she'd grown another couple of heads, so she must have done *something*. Sighing, Izzy tried to make peace.

"You're right. I'm sorry. I don't feel so great. Tell Kara not to bother with the tea, OK? You guys go – maybe I'll catch up with you later?"

"You're not coming?" Juliet asked. Tigs was already stalking towards the door, barking for Kara.

"I think I'm just going to go back to bed," Izzy said with a shrug.

"If you're sure…"

"Definitely. And thanks, by the way. For bringing me home."

And just like that, they were gone, leaving Izzy alone in the apartment.

She leaned her forehead against the door as she locked it behind them. She wouldn't normally bother – after all, there were only two other flats on the landing and anyone else coming up had to be buzzed into the lift lobby by the porter. But somehow, today, it felt like the door needed to be locked. The same went for the windows, despite the rising heat. She went from room to room, yanking the curtains closed against the sun … but somehow that only made it worse. The whole apartment felt too hot, too claustrophobic and too empty at the same time. It was suffocating.

"Nope," she said to nobody in particular. "Just no." She couldn't stay there, no matter how much she wanted to.

Grabbing her bag, she unlocked the door again and stepped out on to the landing.

Ten minutes later, Izzy was in the middle of the Barbican Centre, handing over the money for a large cappuccino from the coffee bar in the main foyer. Even though it was a big space, with different levels and balconies filled with comfortable cushioned benches or tables and chairs, it was buzzing with life. People were coming and going, on their way in or out. Some were heading to the box office to buy tickets for the cinema or the theatre. There were a bunch of kids with their teacher, obviously on their last class trip before they broke up for the summer, too. There were people moving in and out of the restaurant, browsing the bookshop and heading into the library. It was just what she'd needed. To be around people, but not actually *with* them.

The experience in the Tube station had left Izzy unsettled. Uneasy. What, exactly, had she seen? What had happened there – and how come none of the others had seen it? And it wasn't just that, was it?

There had been everything else – the garden, Juliet's house, her own apartment...

She shivered, clutching her coffee more tightly.

Not really wanting to go home, Izzy sat on one of the cushioned benches that dotted the foyer and flicked through a magazine someone had left behind. She carried on flipping until the school kids had left, and what remained of her coffee had gone cold. There was music playing somewhere in the Centre – something discordant (the kind her dad liked to call "modern nonsense"). It was full of jangling bells that set her teeth on edge the longer she listened. She did feel better, though, in spite of the music. There had been no more shadows moving out of the corner of her eye. No more mysterious figures running about, and definitely no more melty faces. This could only be a plus. Even so, she didn't fancy walking back through (or even past) the gardens.

Instead of taking the main doors out on to the terrace, she headed towards the ramp that sloped up and round to the back of the Barbican Centre, flattening out into another of the covered walkways that ran around the complex and emerged at the base of Shakespeare Tower. She could see if Tigs was still around, maybe catch up with the others if she was lucky. Avoiding the gardens meant it would take her almost twice as long to get there, but it was worth it. And besides, this way looped past her favourite part of the whole Centre – the windows on to the Barbican Theatre's wardrobe department. When the lights were on inside, anyone walking past could look in and see the racks of costumes for whichever play happened to be in residence. Sometimes it would be sumptuous fairytale gowns and jackets, each with a white-powdered wig sitting on a stand above it. At other times it would be rows of suits in every possible shade of grey. Last Christmas, she'd stood on the walkway and almost choked with laughter watching the costume fitting for the pantomime's cow.

Today, however, as she drew close to the windows, she could see that the lights were off. There were no costumes lined up in front of the window; none of the staff were trying to iron out the creases from last night's performance or to sew on missing beads. Everything was in darkness.

The walkway swept around, past the windows – and as she walked past the third and final one, she realized with a start that there was someone inside after all. She could see movement in the gloom. A cleaner, maybe, or an assistant running in to fetch something and in too much of a hurry to switch on the lights.

There was something about the movement, though, that made her stop. It was jerky, repetitive. The harder she looked, the more she was convinced she could see the outline of a person, but rather than moving about the room they stayed in one spot. Izzy frowned, peering in through the window. Whoever it was, all they were doing was shaking their head from side to side – and doing it fast. Faster than she'd seen anyone ever do it.

Faster than anyone should be able to do it...

Sweat prickled between her shoulder blades, and the cool of the concrete walkway started to feel like a chill.

Izzy walked on, telling herself that it was nothing. Another trick of the light. A fan, perhaps, switched on in the darkness to cool the room.

Not a person. It couldn't be a person. No one could move their head like that – not really.

And she had almost convinced herself when she heard the first of the footsteps behind her.

Chapter Six

At first, she thought it was someone walking the same way she was, maybe to one of the theatre offices that opened off the walkway. After all, lots of people went along it every day. People just like her. Normal, everyday, average people. Not creepy stalker-types or anything. It was *fine*.

Except that when she stopped, the footsteps stopped, too. And when she walked faster, they sped up along with her.

"Idiot," she muttered to herself. "They're *your* footsteps." She'd been freaked out by an echo. To prove it to herself, she stopped again. The footsteps stopped.

She hopped three steps.

The footsteps did not.

Trying to get over the fact that she'd just randomly hopped down the walkway in front of a complete stranger – who doubtless now thought she was a total weirdo – Izzy stopped and bent down as if to adjust a shoe.

The footsteps stopped, too.

Izzy's breath caught in her throat.

Someone *was* following her.

She had a choice. She could turn and face them, or she could run.

Panic flashed through her. There'd been that safety talk at school a couple of months ago. And why couldn't she remember any of it? That was right – she'd been trying to get that English essay finished, hadn't she? At the time, it had seemed more important than listening to how to deal with a hypothetical stalker. So *that* had been a good call, clearly.

There'd been something about staying calm. Sure. Staying calm and slowing down. That was it – slow down, turn around. Never run. Never lose control.

Slowly, she stood up. Her knees felt weak, as though the smallest gust of wind would break them. But she stood up anyway, and she fought against the rising tide of fear that was flooding her chest, her throat, making it impossible to breathe. She fought against it and she took as deep a breath as she could – and she turned round to look down the walkway behind her.

There was no one there.

The walkway was completely deserted, there wasn't a soul in sight. None of the office doors showed any sign of having been opened – the mystery walker hadn't just stepped through one, surely? Everything was completely still, completely silent.

Izzy stared back along the empty passage. "I'm going mad. It's finally happened." She shook her head. It had to have been an echo after all, distorted by the curving concrete of the walls.

She started walking again, and the footsteps started up behind her. The hairs on the back of her neck stood up. But it was nothing, she told herself. Nothing. She'd checked.

She stumbled slightly, her shoe scuffing the clay tiles of the floor.

The footsteps sped up.

Izzy couldn't even begin to convince herself it was an echo now – and she couldn't just walk calmly as though nothing was happening. This was wrong. It was all *wrong*. She walked faster, until she was half walking, half jogging. But the footsteps behind her kept going at the pace they had before.

A sudden, desperate hope came to her, that

someone was playing a trick on her – following her, and then darting into an alcove or doorway every time she stopped. It was Tigs or Dom, or even just a random stranger. Someone wanting to mess with her head. Without breaking her stride or slowing down, and definitely not stopping, she whipped around again, and carried on walking, facing back the way she had come. She was totally alone but, to her horror, the footsteps stayed with her. If anything, they seemed to be getting closer – they sounded harder, more purposeful. Deliberate, as if whoever was making them was now only a couple of paces away from her and was stretching out with an unseen hand…

Her shoulder collided with something solid behind her, and she couldn't stop herself from screaming. The sound of the footsteps vanished as she tumbled to the ground – and Izzy looked up to see Grey staring back down at her. He must have been coming the other way, and she'd managed to crash straight into him.

He looked just as shocked as she did. But it was more than that – he looked *terrible*. His skin was greasy and sallow, and there were dark circles under his eyes. His hair hung lankly over his face.

"Sorry, did I scare you?" he asked as Izzy picked herself up.

She shook her head. "No. It's…" She tailed off. It would sound ridiculous if she said it out loud – that she'd been running away from phantom footsteps. Because that was something crazy people did. "It's nothing. You look awful, by the way."

"Thanks." He ruffled his hair with his fingers, but it didn't do any good. He still looked just as bad. "Not seen you for a couple of days. Not since—"

"Juliet's party?" She cut him off. "Yeah. I wanted to crash out on the sofa for a while."

"Not feeling very sociable?"

"Not particularly. It just felt like such an effort, seeing people."

"Wow. Thanks." He grinned, pretending to be offended.

"Not you. Obviously. You're not people."

"Again – *thanks*."

"Anyway." It was time to change the subject, she clearly wasn't doing herself *any* favours carrying on this way. "What happened to you, then?" If she kept talking, he might not notice the crazy. She could always hope.

"Rough night, you know?"

"One?"

"*Really* rough night."

"Tell me about it," she said with a sigh as they fell into step, just as they always did — although today things felt a little different. "I feel like I've not slept in weeks."

"Me neither. But last night was definitely the wo—" He stopped abruptly. "Iz?"

"Mmm."

"How many weeks, exactly?"

"What?"

"How long do you think it's been?"

"Since what?"

"I don't know… Since you got a decent night's sleep, maybe? Or at least felt like you did?"

"God, I don't even remember. Before the exams, I guess. I'm kind of hoping everything'll get back to normal, now they're done." Izzy shrugged. He was peering at her, but wasn't really seeing her. He was looking through her, somehow. "You're thinking, aren't you? It shows."

"Since the exams." Apparently he wasn't hearing her, either. Or at least not properly. "How about since the end of term – the start of study leave?"

Izzy shrugged. "Something like that. It's not exactly shocking, though, is it? Not after all the 'You must pass your exams or your life's *over…*' stuff."

"I'm not joking."

"You're an idiot. An idiot who clearly needs to go back to bed."

"Izzy." He was looking at her now, looking at her properly. She looked back at him. His eyes were red; the shadows under them were bruised shades of blue and purple and green. "I know exactly when this started. It started the first night we took those pills."

"The study aid? Oh, come on."

"Izzy, listen. It's not just me. Noah called me this morning – he said Dom's freaking out about something."

"About what?"

"He says he keeps seeing things."

"You mean like the other night?" The conversation was starting to make Izzy uncomfortable. After all, hadn't she seen something then, too?

"I don't know. He thinks he's being followed. They're going over to Tigs's place later to … I dunno,

'Talk About It' or whatever."

"That'll make her happy…"

"This is serious, Iz. Something's not right."

And however much she wanted to argue with him, deep down Izzy knew that she couldn't. Because however much she wanted to ignore it, however much she wanted to pretend, something was very, very wrong.

Izzy thought back to the last time they were gathered in Tigs's apartment. Only Kara was missing, and they were all sitting in the same places … but the mood couldn't have been more different. That time, they were tense – the exams were looming over them like a cliff. This time? This time, the exams were done. The exams were done and they were scared. There was no other way of saying it. Instead of joking and laughing as they had before, everyone looked twitchy. Everyone, thought Izzy as she glanced around, looked *tired*. How had they changed so much in just a couple of days? All of them had shadows under their eyes. Even Tigs, now she was looking more closely. The signs were well hidden under carefully applied make-up, but they were there. How had she not noticed it earlier? Maybe because then she'd been more worried about whether she was going crazy. Now, though…

Dom looked the worst. His eyes were bloodshot, his cropped dark hair greasy. He slumped in the corner of the sofa, worrying at a thread on his board shorts, barely speaking or looking up. Barely even awake.

"But he was fine yesterday," Juliet was saying, as Izzy and Grey walked in.

"He's not fine now, though, is he?" said Noah. He peered at Dom, who blinked slowly.

"What happened?" Izzy looked at Mia, who shook her head, not taking her eyes off her twin.

"I don't know. We were just at home last night and Mum was out, and I went upstairs to take a shower. And, like, five minutes later he's banging on the bathroom door saying there's some guy outside the flat trying to get in."

"In the corridor?" Juliet asked.

"On the balcony."

"What, just standing there and looking in?" Something about the direction the conversation was taking made Izzy uncomfortable.

"I know!"

"What did you do?"

"I got out the shower and went to see."

"And?"

"Nobody there. I swear, I had my phone and I was literally about to call the police – the way Dom was freaking out, you'd think there was a serial killer out there or something." Mia sighed. "*Apparently*, by the time I got there, the guy had just done a runner along the balcony." It was blindingly obvious that not only did Mia not believe her brother, she thought he was either going mad or lying – or both.

Dom looked up, blinking slowly. "He was there. I'm telling you, he was there."

"And then what? He just vanished? Yeah, right."

"He did! I swear!"

"So what did he look like, then? If you saw him so well? And how come none of the neighbours complained about some guy shoving past *their* windows?" Mia folded her arms across her chest and waited. Everyone was watching them. No one else knew what to say – or quite what was happening.

Dom just hung his head again. "It was dark."

That was all he could manage, and he slumped back into the sofa cushions. Mia pulled an I-told-you-so face. Everyone just stared at Dom. Everyone except for Tigs.

The whole time Dom and Mia had been talking, Tigs had gazed out of the window. Now she was examining her fingernails. If she was aiming for 'couldn't care less', she'd hit the mark and then some. While everybody else was worried about Dom, she looked like she was much more interested in her nail polish. After what felt like forever, she turned away from the window.

"This is all great, but what exactly does it have to do with the rest of us?"

"Tigs!" said Juliet, but Tigs just shot her a death-stare.

Juliet shut up again.

"Seriously, what does this have to do with anyone? Dom's having some kind of mental meltdown. Whatever." She waved a hand dismissively. "And anyway, why did it have to be *here*? Today's just been such a bust. First there was her little 'episode' this morning…" She glared at Izzy, who felt her face turning red. "And now this. I mean, Jesus. It's the summer. All the stress is supposed to be *over*?"

Izzy could feel Grey staring at her. She looked at

him, and saw him mouthing "Episode?".

She shook her head slightly. It could wait until later.

He watched her for a moment longer, then scrunched up his nose like he always did when he'd made up his mind.

"You know why we had to meet here?" he said, raising his voice. He sounded hoarse. "It had to be here because this is where it started."

"What's that supposed to mean?" In the bright light beside the window, the shadows under Tigs's eyes were clearer.

"It means that this is where we took those stupid pills of yours." Grey looked at each of the others in turn. "How are you guys sleeping lately, by the way? You tired? Having nightmares? Maybe you wake up in the morning feeling like you haven't slept at all?"

Tigs's face twisted into a sneer. "The *study* pills? Are you kidding me? Dom's gone off the deep end and you're going to blame it on a bunch of *vitamins*?"

"Vitamins! You're still sticking with that, are you?" Grey laughed.

Everyone looked at him.

"What are you saying?" Juliet asked. If anything, Izzy thought she'd got even paler since they'd walked in.

"I'm saying…" Grey stopped and sighed. "I'm saying … *what the hell was in those pills?*"

Chapter Seven

There was a shocked silence in the room. Everyone looked from Grey to Tigs and back again because, honestly, that was the question none of them had wanted to ask. They'd all been thinking it, though – it showed on their faces. Izzy had thought it every single time she'd taken one of the foul-tasting yellow pills. She'd thought it … and each time, she'd decided that the exam results were more important than knowing. The results were what counted – being good, being better, being the best. *That* was the only thing that counted. No matter what the consequences might be.

"What was in the pills, Tigs?" Grey repeated.

Tigs didn't answer. She just stared at him, her lips set in an angry line.

"What was in the pills, Tigs?" he asked again. He obviously wasn't going to stop.

She was still staring him down, but Izzy could see

the corners of her mouth softening, see her bottom lip starting to wobble.

The unthinkable was about to happen. Antigone Price, of all people, was about to cry. The ice queen's frosty exterior had cracked. She slumped on to the chair – Noah stepped out of the way, his eyes wide, as Tigs buried her face in her hands. "I don't know, all right?" she wailed.

"What does that mean?" Juliet asked.

Tigs glared up at her, then dropped her head back into her hands. "It means I don't know, all right? They're just supposed to be…"

"*Supposed* to be?" Dom leaned forward on the sofa. Beads of sweat glistened on his forehead. "What are they *supposed* to be, Tigs? What did you give us?" He spat the words at her.

Izzy had seen enough. "How about we all just calm down?" she said, stepping into the middle of the room. It felt like standing in a thundercloud.

"How about we don't?" Dom shouted back at her. His face was twisted, furious. He jumped up and took a step towards her, but Mia followed him and grabbed his elbow, pulling him back to the sofa.

"Dom! Would you sit down and shut up? Before

you *fall* down?" Mia tugged on his elbow and Dom collapsed back into the cushions of the sofa, blinking groggily.

Grey folded his arms across his chest. "Noah?" he said quietly. His voice was hoarse, but calm again.

Noah cleared his throat. "Tigs…" he said, more gently than Izzy had been expecting. Tigs's bottom lip was still wobbling, and either she was doing a really good job of holding everything together or, more likely, she'd never been that close to bursting into tears in the first place. After all, it *was* Tigs.

Tigs looked up and Noah carried on. "Where *exactly* did you get those pills from?"

"I told you, the same place my mother gets all her stuff from!" She glared at him and wiped her nose with the back of her hand.

"Yeah. About that…" Noah fiddled with his sandy brown hair, looking uncomfortable. Izzy froze. What was going on? She shot Grey a look but he blanked her, his attention completely fixed on Noah. "You sure?"

"Of course I'm sure!" Tigs snarled back at him, slapping her hand on the cushion next to her for emphasis. It had taken less than a minute for her to go from wounded and tearful to outraged.

Neither appeared to work on Noah. "Well, they're not there now." He jabbed at the screen on his phone, then held it out to Tigs. Jumping up, she snatched it from his hand and stared at the screen.

"So? They're out of stock or something. Seriously, I don't know what—"

"They never had them, according to the email I got." Noah raised his voice slightly to make himself heard over Tigs. She stopped, shoving his phone back at him.

"What?"

"I said, not according to the mail I got from the customer service team. They've never heard of them, and they never stocked anything even vaguely similar."

"But that's stupid. Of course they did ... do." She scooped up her expensive bag and started to rummage through it for her own phone. After a moment or two of searching, she sighed and dropped the bag back on to the floor. The soft leather made a quiet *huffff* sound as it landed, almost as though it was sighing. "I'll show you," Tigs said as she stalked out of the room, only to reappear clutching an iPad with a bright pink cover. She slid her finger across the screen and poked at it several times with a finger. The tablet made a clicking noise as she tapped in an address and skimmed through the pages of a website. The expression on her face changed from anger to surprise to confusion. "Oh," she said, and her voice sounded small. She sat down and shook her head. More tapping. More scrolling.

"Oh…" again. Then – "I don't get it." Tigs looked up, her eyes moving from one to another of them, around the room. "There was a page on the site. With … stuff. And it's gone." More clicking.

"Like I said…" Noah began, but Tigs held up her hand to cut him off. Obediently, he shut up. It was a force of habit – when Tigs wanted you to stop talking, you stopped talking.

"I had an email, like an order confirmation thing? It's gone. And there was this other one – the email I got before that said they had this new product in… That's how I found them in the first place!" Stricken, she looked at Noah. "How can it be gone? How can it all be gone?"

"Let me look." He held out his hand and dutifully she handed him the iPad. He perched on the arm of the sofa, scrolling and frowning.

Eventually, Mia sighed. "You want to tell us what all this is actually *about*?"

"I don't quite know," Noah said, shaking his head. "It's like the pills don't exist. Anywhere. At all." He passed the iPad back to Tigs.

"But that's not possible!" Izzy couldn't keep up. From where she stood, it sounded like Noah was saying every trace of FokusPro had been removed – not just from the site where Tigs claimed she'd bought it, but even from her email account.

"Tigs, are you absolutely sure you bought them from that site?" Noah's voice was stern.

"Of course I'm sure. It's not like I'm just going to go and buy a load of pills from some random site, is it?"

"Tigs. This is serious."

"I *know*!" Tigs rolled her eyes. "I get it, OK? But I'm telling you, that's where the pills came from and that's who sent me an email to confirm it. How can the email have gone?"

"You use webmail. It's not impossible to hack the servers and delete something…" Noah shrugged. "But it's unlikely. I mean, I don't see why—"

Dom sat forward. "It's *them*."

"Them who?" Noah asked, turning to face him.

"Them. The watchers."

"Oh, God. Here we go again…" Mia groaned. "Enough, already. There's nobody *watching* us, all right?"

"The man on the balcony. The man in the gardens…" Dom was on his feet again, spinning to face each of them in turn. "Don't you see? Juliet…" he pointed at her, his eyes wide and bloodshot. Juliet shrank back into the sofa cushions. "There *was* someone in your house. They were watching us. They're after the pills. They want them back. They know!"

"Dom … what…?" Juliet tried, and even from across the room, Izzy could see the confusion on her face, the fear, but it was no use.

"We need to tell someone. We have to stop them. We have to. Have to. They're watching us. They know!" He was wheeling crazily where he stood, spinning and spinning as the others looked on in horror. Izzy tore her gaze away from him and flashed another look at Grey. This time, she caught his eye and saw the same panic in his face that she knew was in hers.

Dom needed help.

It was, as always, Mia who stepped in. "Enough, bro. I'm taking you home." She lunged forward and grabbed at Dom, who was still spinning wildly. She caught him just as he staggered sideways, bumping into the sideboard near the door. A row of delicate glass bottles arranged on the top wobbled dangerously. "Home. Now." And without another word, Mia dragged Dom out into the hall.

Everyone else just stared at each other.

"Wow." Izzy sank into the empty space left on the sofa by Mia and Dom. "Dom's really losing it."

"He's not the only one," Tigs sniffed, looking pointedly from Izzy to Noah.

Grey frowned. "Tigs…"

"What the hell's going on?" Tigs turned on Grey. "You're standing there looking at me like I've done something wrong. Like you didn't take the pills, too?"

"Of course I took them! We all took them, didn't we?"

"Everyone but Kara," Juliet whispered.

"And look how that turned out for *her*," Tigs snapped back.

"Yeah, well." Juliet fiddled with her necklace, wrapping the fine gold chain round and round her finger. She peered over the top of her glasses at everyone. "What *is* all this about, anyway?"

Noah shrugged. "Something's not right. I went to look into the FokusPro, and it's pretty much like you just saw – they don't exist. They've vanished from the internet. Completely."

Something niggled at the back of Izzy's mind. A nagging idea. She opened and closed her mouth once, thinking better of saying it out loud, but then decided that it was probably worth it, anyway.

"Noah ... why were you looking for them?"

"I... What?" Noah looked crestfallen.

"Good point!" Tigs swivelled in her seat. "Why were you?"

Noah glanced at Grey, then stuffed his hands in his pockets. "I was looking for more." His voice was heavy with defeat.

"Noah!" Izzy couldn't help it. She was shocked. Noah, of all people. Noah, the smartest of them all by a mile. "You were trying to find more of the FokusPro? Why?"

"Why'd you think? They work."

"But the exams are over. Why would you need more? I thought it was just supposed to be this one..."

Izzy tailed off, but Noah had already figured out what she was going to say.

He grinned at her. "You know as well as I do that there's always more exams, Iz. I'm on a scholarship, remember? I can't afford to blow this – like, I *literally* can't afford it. The pills just seemed like they'd … be a useful safety net."

"I didn't mean… It's not…" Her face flushed – she could feel the heat of it climbing from the neck of her T-shirt up towards her cheeks.

"I know what you meant." His face grew serious. "But that isn't the point."

"So what is?"

"This is." He reached down to his bag and pulled out his laptop, setting it on the table. "Tigs might not be able to use the internet properly, but I can." He leaned over the computer and calmly pressed a button, turning the whole thing round so that the screen was facing into the room. He dropped into a chair next to the table and folded his arms across his chest.

"Watch. You'll see."

A black rectangle filled the screen. There was something written at the bottom in functional white text – a string of numbers and letters, and what looked like a date — but it was gone too quickly for Izzy to make it all out. Something about July? The caption dissolved into the screen, which was suddenly replaced by blurry black and white footage, the kind of thing she'd seen on CCTV and surveillance programmes on television. Like the others, she stared at it, trying to work out exactly what it was she was seeing.

The footage was of a small, square room. It was sparsely furnished and brightly lit. It looked clinical, somehow. There was a narrow metal bed, which appeared to be bolted to the floor. A dressing table with an empty frame that had obviously once held a mirror above it. A small, wooden stool in front of it — again, bolted to the floor. There were no windows and only one door, with a tiny barred hatch cut into it at head height. There was no door handle.

The image remained static for what felt like an age. Nothing moved. And then, suddenly, there was a shadow on the far side of the bed that hadn't been there before. Izzy held her breath as a figure slid out from beneath the bed and stood up. It was a man. He was wearing a kind of pale-coloured jumpsuit, and he had a long, matted beard. His hair was curly and bushy – it stuck out wildly from his head. He stood with a slight stoop, and for a moment it looked like he was waving his hand up and down alongside his face, until Izzy realized that he was scratching. It was just that his nails were so long, he didn't need to touch his skin with his fingers.

She glanced at Noah. He was watching her – watching all of them – watching the video on the screen.

"Keep watching," he whispered.

"What is this?"

"Keep watching."

She turned her eyes back to the screen.

The man in the room was still scratching; still running his long nails down one side of his face. Even on the grainy camera footage, Izzy could see three long gouges beginning to appear on his cheek where his nails dug into his flesh. Blood trickled down his jaw, splashing on the shoulder of his jumpsuit.

Movement on the other side of the screen caught Izzy's eye. The door was opening and a man and a woman walked in. She was wearing a suit, he was wearing what looked like a uniform. Something vaguely military, Izzy guessed, although even on a less grainy picture she wouldn't have been able to tell exactly what.

The suited woman hurried over to the original occupant of the room, who was still standing there, idly tearing at his face, and pulled his hand down. He didn't appear to notice. She steered him to the bed and sat him down on the edge of the mattress. He sat quietly, staring ahead with his hands in his lap as the man in uniform paced. Izzy guessed he was talking. The woman looked at him for a moment, nodded and then left the room. She closed the door behind her.

It was hard to watch what happened next, but every time she tried to look away, Izzy found Noah scowling at her. "You need to see."

The uniformed man talked and paced and talked and paced. Then he talked and paced some more. But he wasn't the one Izzy was watching. It was the man in the jumpsuit. At first, he sat motionless, his hands still folded in his lap. Then his head twitched to the side, just once. The uniformed man was still pacing up and down.

Another head twitch.

A couple of fingers jerking.

Another twitch of his head, which ran into another and into another until he was shaking his head from side to side so violently that even the man in the uniform stopped what he was doing and moved over to him, putting a hand on his shoulder as if to restrain him.

The man in the jumpsuit stopped. And sank his teeth into the other's hand.

Even as the military man recoiled, pulling back and away, the prisoner leaped at him. He hit him with such ferocity that they both tumbled to the floor, rolling over and over. Until they stopped, and something liquid and dark began to pool beneath them, spreading slowly outwards.

Across the room the door was thrown open and the woman rushed back in. She was carrying a bundle of fabric straps that trailed on the floor behind her.

The man in the jumpsuit – the prisoner, or whatever he was – rocked back on to his heels and snarled at her. His face twisted as she stopped dead halfway across the room. The bundle of restraints spooled on to the floor. She didn't stand a chance.

The video dissolved into a snowstorm of static, but all Izzy could see was that final image of the man in the jumpsuit throwing himself at the woman. And her final desperate look straight into the camera.

"What did we just see?" Grey was the first to speak, and when he did he sounded shaken.

"That?" Noah closed the lid of his laptop. "That's what happened to the last guy who took FokusPro."

No one said anything else while that really sank in. Finally, Juliet spoke. "I think I'm going to be sick. Is this some kind of joke?"

"I don't know, Jools. You reckon?"

"I think I'm going to be sick," she repeated.

Izzy watched as Grey leaned against the wall, rubbing his face with the heels of his hands. It was an unpleasant echo of the man in the video scratching at his cheek.

If Noah was right, and he usually was, then getting caught was suddenly looking like the least of their problems.

They drifted away, one at a time, back to their homes. Nobody looked anyone else in the eye as they made their excuses and left. Izzy's legs felt weak, the way they did after she'd watched a really good horror film for the first time, but then, the shakes were always part of the fun. This wasn't fun. This was … something else. Her feet were heavy and slow, and the walk back to Lauderdale seemed to take a week. She wished she'd waited for Grey, but he'd been so deep in thought and she guessed that he hadn't seen her leave. As she stepped out of the lift up to her floor, she almost fell right over the bags on the landing. She groaned as she recognized them – they were her dad's. Frankfurt. He must be leaving today.

The door to their apartment was ajar. From inside, she could hear the noise of him busily packing and moving around. She could hear the hard soles of his shoes clicking across the kitchen floor. Pacing.

He was waiting for her to come home, wasn't he?

"Any other day, Dad," Izzy muttered under her breath, but there was no way round it. She blew out a long breath and smoothed down her hair, hoping she looked better than she felt, before pushing open the door.

"There you are! I was worried I'd missed you." He hurried into the hall, dropping a kiss on the top of her head. "I know I said I was flying out tomorrow, but one of the directors has asked us to head out tonight — something about a dinner with the guys from the front office."

As usual, everything he said about his work went right over Izzy's head. She'd learned a long time ago that it was usually best to smile and nod, even though he might as well have been speaking in Dutch.

"I stocked up for you. There's food in the fridge and the freezer, and there's cash in the pot by the phone if you need it..."

"Dad..."

"I know, I know. You can look after yourself."

"Dad..."

"And don't forget, the cleaner's due. But can you ask her to leave my study this time? It's full of paperwork and I..." He tailed off as he actually looked at her. "Are you feeling all right? You look terrible. Do you need me to give the surgery a ring before I—"

"Dad, I'm fine. I just wanted to say have a nice trip and don't *worry*." She gave him her best smile. "Good luck with the project."

"Izzy, is everything OK?" His forehead creased into a series of parallel worry-lines. "I worry about you, yes. But the exams... I know how hard it's been, how hard you've worked and—"

"It's fine. I didn't sleep well last night; think I'm going to go to bed early, you know?"

"You're sure?"

"You'll miss your flight." She took the smile up a notch. The lower half of her face felt like it was going to fall off.

"I've got loads of… Ah." He looked at his watch. "Maybe not…" In a single move, he swept his phone off the hall shelf and into his jacket pocket, scooped up his passport and his wallet and picked up his laptop bag. "It's only three nights and I'll be back, OK? You have any problems, you call me. It doesn't matter what time it—"

"*Dad!* Go!" Izzy handed him the file that was sitting beside the phone and bundled him out of the door. She watched as he gathered his bags up from the lobby floor and hauled them all into the lift with a nod back at her. She heard his voice floating back as the lift closed on him, calling, "Love you!"

As the lift whirred, taking him down to the lobby and away, Izzy rested her head against the wood of the doorframe. It had been a hard choice in the end – harder than she'd expected. When she had seen his things on the landing, seen the door open and heard his shoes, all she'd wanted to do was tell him. Tell him about the pills, about Tigs, about Noah. About the figure in the gardens, about Dom. About the scene in the Tube station, about the footsteps, about the video.

But when it came down to it, she couldn't. As she'd opened her mouth – even as she'd started to speak – she had heard Noah's voice in her head again. She couldn't afford to blow this, either. She'd seen Mrs Alderman sitting at the desk at the front of the classroom; she'd seen her dad sitting beside her in the head's office of her old school, heard him defending her. He'd even made a donation to the school's new science lab fund – and a sizeable one at that – just so that everyone could "move on with no hard feelings".

All she wanted was to show him it had all been worth it; to show him *she'd* been worth it. To make him proud. It had taken a year for her to convince him she was fine, that everything was going to be OK. He trusted her. She'd promised him he *could* trust her. She couldn't exactly turn around and tell him that she'd let him down again, could she?

It was no good. The FokusPro (and everything that came with it) was her secret. And that was how it was going to have to stay.

Chapter Eight

Izzy lay on her bed. She'd counted sheep. She'd counted dust motes wheeling in the sunshine as she stared up at the ceiling. She'd picked at a loose thread on the edge of her pillow, only to realize that if she pulled it, the whole end of her pillowcase would start to unravel. She'd stopped picking at it. Somehow, the apartment felt emptier than usual, as though just knowing her dad wouldn't be back for a couple of days made him less present than he had been for the last week. It wasn't like she'd seen much of him lately, but there was something more definite about his absence now. Maybe because he was on a plane rather than a few minutes' walk away. But he was right – it was only for a few days and she was used to it, after all.

Hours passed. She'd tried to read. She'd tried to listen to music, the radio, podcasts.

She'd even just tried closing her eyes and hoping it would get her to sleep, but every time she did, she saw a crazed man clawing at a terrified woman and heard footsteps creeping closer to her bed. Once or twice, she was on the edge of dozing off, but as she sank deeper into almost-sleep she started awake again, convinced she had heard something – a thud, like a door being slammed shut. The first time, she actually got up from her bed and went to check that it wasn't the kitchen window banging against its latch. Thirteen floors up, the last thing anyone wants is a broken window showering glass everywhere. Everything seemed to be normal, and the noise was probably just builders somewhere in the tower. With as many flats stacked on top of each other as there were, someone else's building work was almost always reverberating through the reinforced concrete.

Only slightly reassured, Izzy went back to staring at the ceiling as the light faded to dusk. She watched as the orange city night-time sky changed to the salmon-pink of early morning. The building work, wherever it was, stopped and started again. The lift pinged as one of the neighbours on their landing came home from work – and, after what felt like an eternity, pinged again as they went back out in the morning. On the road below, right at the edge of the Barbican, taxis hooted.

And still Izzy didn't sleep.

By the time the sun was bright in the sky it was obvious that she wasn't going to, so she dragged herself out of bed and did the things she always did in the morning. Shower, coffee, all the same as usual. But the smell of the toast she made for breakfast turned her stomach and she dropped it into the waste disposal unit without taking a single bite. She stared out of the windows. She tried to watch television, but found her eyes refused to focus on the screen; instead, they drifted to a blank spot on the wall. It took so much effort to look away that she gave up, and stared at the wall.

The video kept replaying itself in her head. The stark room with its bolted-down bed. The patient … prisoner. The woman. Over and over again. What had happened? Where were they? *Who* were they? Noah had said he found it online – perhaps there were more answers.

Izzy stumbled back to her room and opened her laptop, collapsing on to the bed with it. She blinked at the screen. Where should she start? It wasn't like the video would be on YouTube, was it? What would she search for? 'Crazy man pills murder'? Idly, she started looking for FokusPro – not really expecting to find it. She didn't. She found lots of videos of cats falling off furniture, a celebrity feud splashed across a dozen websites and a pair of shoes on sale that Juliet had been eyeing up for weeks. But no pills.

By lunchtime, she was practically climbing the walls. Even stepping out on to the balcony she didn't feel like she was getting any air – just lungs full of warm exhaust fumes from the traffic below. Picking up a book, she decided to go and sit in the garden by the lake for a while. Being out in the sunshine was exactly what she needed, Izzy thought as she pressed the button for the lift.

Inside, the steel walls of the lift were polished to a shine and Izzy could see her reflection, twisted and distorted, looking back at her as she stepped inside. The lift had barely started to move before it juddered to a stop with a screech.

The lights flickered. Then went out.

She was plunged into almost total blackness – the only light was the soft red glow from behind the lift buttons, illuminating the floor numbers.

"It's fine. It's just a power glitch. That's all," she said to herself. Her voice bounced off the metal walls.

There was an ominous creak above and, even in the darkness, Izzy found herself looking up. Her heart was pounding in her throat and it was all she could do not to whimper.

Lifts had alarm buttons, didn't they? That's what you were supposed to do if the lift stopped. You pressed the alarm. She looked at the buttons arranged in two neat columns, glowing gently. Right at the bottom, all by itself, was the one she wanted – smaller, and marked with a stylized bell. She reached for it, but her fingertip had barely brushed the surface when she yanked her hand away and dropped her book.

The button was wet.

It was sticky. Warm.

Rubbing her fingers and thumb together, she could feel it on her skin. Was it oil? Was something leaking from the mechanism above her?

Slowly, carefully, she raised her hand towards her face. The smell hit her almost immediately – it was coppery, and somehow meaty. It reminded her of…

No. It didn't just remind her. It *was*.

Blood.

She looked again at the lift buttons. The red backlighting was still there, still glowing, but the edges of the numbers had blurred. Even as she watched, they smudged together, smearing into a single shining red panel. She could see it seeping down the wall, hear it dripping on to the floor.

She stepped back, trying to put as much distance between her and the blood-soaked wall as possible. Her feet stuck to the floor as the blood began to pool around her toes, seeping into the carpet, into her shoes. She could feel a scream beginning to climb up into her throat...

The lift was moving again. The lights were back on.

The lights were back on and she was wedged into the corner of the lift, her back to the walls.

She sucked down the air, gulping it into her lungs, trying to swallow the light and drive out the darkness as though it would wash away the image of the blood...

Looking down, the floor was clean. The walls of the lift were clean. There was no blood, no nothing. Only her book, lying innocently in the middle of the carpet tiles.

The lift slowed and there was a *ping* as the doors slid open.

Suddenly, Izzy didn't want to go and sit in the garden. She wanted to be in her room, with several locked doors between her and the outside world. The problem was that to get there, she had to get back in the lift. And she couldn't make herself do it.

She tried. She really tried. But every time she pressed the button to call the lift and the doors opened, goosebumps rose all over her skin and her feet simply refused to move.

After a while, the porter stuck his head around the door from the main lobby.

"You OK?" he asked, seeing her leaning against the wall, clutching her book.

"Fine," she squeaked. "Had a bit of a dizzy thing."

"You want me to come up to thirteen with you – make sure you get in all right?"

"Oh, God. Yes. Yes, please," said Izzy, hoping she didn't sound as desperate as she felt.

The porter gave her a slightly odd look, but got into the lift anyway and pressed the button for her floor. Taking a deep breath, she followed him and they stood awkwardly alongside each other. When the doors opened on to her landing, she let out a long sigh of relief. She hadn't realized she'd been holding her breath all the way up.

Izzy waved at the porter, who peered out of the lift at her as she unlocked the door to the apartment and let herself in. She locked the door behind her. Then, without even taking off her shoes, she walked through the hallway and straight into her room, closing the door on the world. And that was where she stayed for the rest of the day – until someone hammered on the front door to the apartment so hard that they almost shook the door off its hinges.

"Izzy! Izzy!"

Even from her bedroom at the far end of the hallway, she could hear Grey shouting her name. Rolling off her bed, feeling more tired than she had ever done before, she ran a hand through her hair to tame it.

"Yeah, yeah," she called as she headed for the door, trying her best to smooth the creases out of her T-shirt. Her phone was lying on the sideboard in the living room. It beeped feebly as she picked it up, carrying it away from the solid walls and into a spot with better signal reception. It beeped again as she opened the door to find Grey staring at her.

"And hello to you, too." She stepped aside as he edged into the hallway.

"Why didn't you answer your phone? I've been going crazy calling you."

"No, you haven't…" Izzy held up the phone in her hand. It beeped one more time and buzzed. A message popped up on the screen, telling her she had seven new voice messages and nine missed calls, all of which came from Grey. "Oops. Left it too close to the wall, I guess. What's up?"

"You mean apart from the fact I've spent most of the day calling you and you don't answer? Apart from *that*, what's up?"

"What's the matter with *you*?" Izzy stared at him. "So I didn't pick up my phone. Big deal."

"Jesus, Izzy." Grey rubbed his hands over his face and leaned against the wall. The back of his head bumped into the edge of a picture frame, knocking it off-centre. And then – "Dom's disappeared. I thought… I thought … something might have happened to you, too."

"What?" Something in Izzy's throat knotted into a cold ball that quickly sank all the way down to her toes, chilling her as it went. "What about Dom?"

"He's gone walkabout. No one can find him and he's not answering his phone. Which makes two of you," he added pointedly.

Izzy flapped a hand at him. "He's probably just gone down to the Centre or something…"

"Yeah, I don't think so. Mia's out of her mind – she's been looking everywhere. Have you heard from him? Have you seen him?"

"Last time I saw either of them, it was at Tigs's. What happened?"

"I don't know. Mia said they were both home this afternoon, and someone knocked on the door with a package for their neighbour. Mia sorted it – and Dom was gone, with the balcony door wide open and all the fire escapes along the balcony open, too. We've been looking for him ever since."

"Why didn't you come find me?"

"I tried calling. A lot."

Izzy pictured the route Dom must have taken. The twins lived in a duplex apartment in Gilbert House, built across the lake with a walkway below it acting as a bridge over the water. Like all the flats in the Barbican, the balcony served as the fire escape route. In Gilbert House, it ran the entire length of the building, divided up by thick glass and metal screens and connecting to the fire stairs at each end.

For someone desperate to run away, it was an easy and obvious escape route. But who had Dom been running from – and where was he going?

"And she's got no idea where he could be?"

"None. You know what those two are like – normally, they're in each other's heads. Not this time. We're going to look for him. Are you coming?"

"Who's *we*?" She ignored the look Grey gave her. "I just don't know if I can handle any more weird stuff…" She tried to make it sound light, unimportant, but the truth was, she meant it. The last few days had been quite enough to freak her out as it was.

"You mean Noah? He's at home, doing more—"

"Research?" She interrupted him. "Because I *love* what he's found so far."

"Hey!" Grey poked her in the shoulder. "Lay off him. What if he's on to something?"

"And what if he's not? I mean, do I need to remind you that the only reason he found out about any of this is because he was looking for more pills?"

"I don't care, OK? What I care about right this minute – now that I know I don't need to be worrying about you – is finding Dom. So are you in or not?"

"Give me a sec. I'll grab my coat."

As she yanked her jacket off the hook in the hall cupboard, she tried her best to ignore the thought that popped into her head while he was speaking.

Should you be worrying about me? Because I am…

"We've already checked the Centre, as well as the library and the cinema. He's not there." Juliet sounded even more miserable than she looked, hunched sadly against one of the giant concrete pillars that supported the structural weight of Gilbert House.

They had met on the bridge over the lake, although there was still no sign of Mia or Tigs, and Noah was apparently doing his hacker thing and chasing down the story of FokusPro. Below them, the surface of the lake was smooth and peaceful, only disturbed by a couple of the resident ducks paddling towards the islands sunk into the water. "You saw the state of him yesterday – he shouldn't be out, never mind wandering round on his own."

"What do you mean?" Izzy swallowed a yawn. It didn't matter how tired she was, she didn't think yawning right now would make her very popular.

"I mean, he can barely walk in a straight line. What happens if he steps out in front of a … a…" Juliet dissolved into tears.

Izzy gave Grey a concerned look – one she could see mirrored on his face. That Juliet was worried was understandable. But even as she spoke, she sounded like she was getting hysterical. It was a bit much, even for her.

"Hey!" The voice came from somewhere beneath them, from the walkway that ran round the edge of the lake. Izzy leaned over one side of the thick wall, Grey over the other. He waved down to someone below, then leaned back again.

"It's Mia. She's going to check the gardens. We should go down and catch up with her."

"I don't want to," said Juliet, sounding small.

"You're still bothered about the gardens?" Grey stared at her. "Isn't that kind of a problem seeing as you basically live there?"

"Thanks for that, Grey. Yes, it's a problem, OK? How do you think I'm sleeping, knowing that there might have been someone watching us? Someone in the house?"

"Probably about as well as the rest of us…" Grey muttered, turning his head away as he spoke.

Juliet half heard him and was about to reply when Izzy cut her off. She could see how this would go.

"Come on," she said, rummaging in her pocket for her key to the gates.

While the lakeside terrace directly outside the Barbican Centre was open to the public, the walkways surrounding the other three sides of the rectangular central lake were only accessible through tall, barred metal gates to which residents alone had the keys, just like the garden. All of the shared stairwells of the blocks around the lake opened out on to the walkways. It was simply a case of finding the right staircase and figuring out which level you needed. Izzy had never been very good at it, and always ended up in either the underground car park or outside someone's front door.

But once Grey had steered Juliet through the door Izzy was holding open, she walked down the stairs on autopilot and they emerged directly across from the Centre, in front of the neat little church that sat beside the lake. The water lapped gently at the edges of the paving, and a duck slid into the lake ahead of them. There was the unmistakable clang of one of the gates closing as Mia headed into the garden. Grey was already hurrying towards the next gate, alongside the girls' school that backed on to the walkway.

The classrooms were deserted, the windows all dark. This section of the walkway was short, with a gate at each end and waist-high railings running alongside the water. Beyond the second gate, the walkway opened on to a fenced-in platform the width of the lake, with yet another gate at each end opening on to either the gardens behind or the lakeside.

As Izzy watched Grey unlock the next gate and heave it open, she realized how like walking through a prison it was navigating the Barbican this way – all locked gates and keys and endless bars. She looked up at the block opposite, hunched at the side of the garden. Behind the bushes, the green-painted metal ventilation grilles from the car park looked like barred windows. From this angle, even the balconies of the upper levels looked like they belonged to some kind of futuristic prison. Despite her jacket and the warmth of the evening, Izzy shivered. And then her eye was caught by a flicker of movement on the raised walkway that overlooked the gardens. For a second, it had almost looked like someone had been watching her. Someone who had ducked out of sight just as she glanced up. She strained her eyes, trying to make them out. It was pointless, but just for a moment...

Another clanging sound brought her back to herself. She had separated from Juliet and Grey without quite realizing it, and was startled to find that not only was she suddenly alone in the enclosed section of the platform, her key was no longer in her hand. And without it, she was trapped.

She stared at her open palm. Her *empty* palm. It had been there a second ago, hadn't it? She'd used it to open the door, then the gate. Or had that been Grey? Had she left her key in the door? In the lock of one of the gates? She ran back to the gate they had come through and pushed her fingers between the metal bars, feeling for the lock. There was no key. She patted down her pockets. Nothing. She looked on the ground. Still nothing.

"Grey!" She couldn't see anyone in the garden. Couldn't hear them either, but surely they hadn't gone far. "Grey!"

No response.

"*Grey!*"

139

There was no reply from Grey, but a sudden rustling sound from the bushes made her freeze.

"Grey?"

The bushes rustled again, and then went quiet.

Izzy took a step back, away from the plants.

A twig snapped, closer this time, and nowhere near the bush that had been moving. Another.

The sun had dipped behind the concrete hulks of the nearest block, and Izzy shivered again, but less from the chill in the air than from fear. One of the larger shrubs in the border was swaying from side to side like someone was shaking it.

Izzy swallowed hard. "Hello?" she called.

The swaying stopped.

"Who's there?"

There was a burst of movement behind the plants. Twigs snapped and branches were shoved aside, leaves scattered. And then nothing.

No one had opened a gate, and there was no way anyone could have climbed over the vents and up the sheer concrete wall to the upper walkway without Izzy having seen them.

And that meant they were still in there with her.

"*Grey!*" She tried again, and this time she shouted

so loudly that her throat hurt. He *had* to hear her now, surely…

But if he did, he didn't reply.

There was absolutely no sound from the bushes or from the garden. Only one part of that was a good thing.

Desperately, Izzy ran back to the gate and wrapped her hands around the bars, shaking the whole thing with every ounce of her strength. It was so heavy, the lock so strong, that it barely even rattled.

And as she let her hands slide from the bars, she heard the first footsteps behind her. Slow at first, tentative, careful. And then heavier. More purposeful. Someone was walking towards her exposed back – and whoever it was, she was locked in there with them.

They came closer and closer and with the sound of every footstep, her skin crawled. The hairs on the back of her neck stood on end as what felt like breath moved across her skin.

She screwed her eyes shut, still unable to bear the thought of turning round.

The creak of metal hinges followed by the sound of a gate slamming snapped her back to the world.

She whirled to face the sound and found herself staring at a small poodle on a lead blinking at her, its head cocked on one side. Holding the other end of the lead was Mrs Johnson from the seventeenth floor. She was standing between the two security gates, a key in her hand.

"Is everything all right, love?" she asked.

Izzy stared mutely back at her and nodded, once. It was the only thing she could think of doing – that, and holding up her hand in a friendly wave.

Her hand that was still clutching the key; clutching it so tightly that the edges had dug deeply enough into the flesh of her palm that they had almost broken the skin.

Her key. In her hand all this time.

Mrs Johnson held the gate into the garden open for her and smiled as she stepped through it and let it close. She gave Izzy another smile and tugged gently on the lead, then set off down the path through the garden, leaving Izzy feeling shaken beside the gate, staring through the metal fencing. There was nobody in there.

As her panic subsided, something began to stir at the back of Izzy's mind. Something like this happening once in a while she could put down to tiredness, to stress. But twice in a couple of days? That couldn't be a coincidence. Could it?

She rested her forehead against one of the black metal bars of the fence. It felt cool, soothing the throb of the headache that was building behind her eyes. She had just about got her pulse back to normal and her panicky shallow breathing under control when she heard a scream rip through the calm evening air from the other side of the lake.

Chapter Nine

The scream echoed off the buildings around the lake, bouncing back from the concrete until it filled the air and seemed to be coming from everywhere all at once. Without even thinking, Izzy doubled back on herself and tore open the gate she had just walked through, back into the cage. Not stopping there, she unlocked the gate directly ahead of her – the one that opened on to the terrace in front of the Barbican Centre. The tables dotted around the terrace were starting to fill up now as people finished work and either came to meet friends for a drink or to see a play or film in the Centre, and several of them were looking around for the source of the scream.

Izzy already knew who it was. It was Mia.

She sprinted across the terrace, opting for the fastest route back around the lake, the one with the fewest gates. Instead of backtracking past the school and church and then under the bridge they'd been on earlier she ran straight across the terrace, leaping the low chain that divided the Barbican's section from what served as the yard of the Guildhall School of Music, and right over to the sole gate on the eastern side of the lake. With shaking hands, she unlocked the gate and wrenched it open.

She could see them now – Grey, Mia, Juliet – but there was no sign of Tigs. They were standing at the top of the steps above the waterfall that cascaded from an industrial concrete half-pipe into this end of the lake, directly in front of Brandon Mews. There was a narrow metal walkway beneath the stairs and the waterfall – a mesh gantry, sunk almost into the water. Long ago, someone had obviously had the bright idea of planting things alongside it, surrounded by the lake, but the space was dark and dingy and the plants were either mostly dead or had turned into long, straggling weedy things that trailed in the water. It was – in spite of the windows overlooking it, most of which were shrouded in net curtains – a hidden place. A secret place. The kind of place where bad things could happen, and nobody would ever know. Izzy had never liked it.

Her foot slipped on the wet metal, sending her

skidding towards the water. She lurched back to catch her balance and smacked the side of her head into the concrete of yet another pillar, this time, one supporting the weight of the stairs above her. Seeing stars, Izzy blinked hard and shook her head to clear it. The sound of the waterfall pouring down all around her turned to a high-pitched whine and then settled back to a dull roar.

And, faintly, the sound of sobbing.

Izzy took the bare concrete stairs two at a time, racing up them until she came to the viewing platform over the waterfall, looking out over the lake and towards the garden. Mia was huddled into Grey, clinging to him with her head pressed deeply into his shoulder. Juliet was a couple of steps away, her face sickly pale. Hearing Izzy come up the stairs, Grey turned his head to see who it was. His lips pressed together in a grim line, and Izzy wished that she hadn't caught his quick downward glance.

Because that's when she saw him.

The floor of the platform was made of the same steel mesh as the walkway, designed to let anyone standing there see the flow of water from above before it gushed over the concrete lip and tumbled into the lake below. Green weed had grown beneath the mesh, waving in the flow of the water. And tangled in it, his eyes staring wildly and sightlessly up from beneath the stream, was Dom.

He was lying face up, his features distorted by the running water and the weed weaving through his hair. One hand was outstretched and limp, drifting towards the surface. He looked blank, somehow. Whatever had made him 'Dom' had gone, and despite the fact that he was wearing exactly the same clothes she'd seen him in last, at Tigs's place, Izzy somehow couldn't quite put the two things together. Dom was Dom. This was a body.

This was Dom's body.

Dom was dead.

Dom was *dead*.

She heard her voice, sounding far away as if it belonged to someone else. "We should call the police."

Grey nodded, dumbly reaching into his pocket for his phone. But as he pulled it out, Mia shook so violently that it slipped out of his hand and fell into the lake with a splash. Grey's shoulders sagged, but given what they were all looking at, a lost phone was hardly their biggest problem.

"He said…" Mia whispered. "He said there was someone, didn't he? And we didn't believe him. I didn't believe him. Why? *Why* didn't I believe him?"

"Mia…" Grey tried, but Mia pushed him away.

"No. I should have listened. I should have…" With a noise that was half yelp, half sob, she spun away from the three of them and fled down the steps.

Juliet made a move to go after her, but Grey shook his head. "No. Let her go."

He blew out a long, sad breath. "Iz? You OK?"

Izzy couldn't tear her eyes away from Dom's water-bleached face. The current caught his hand and it bobbed against the flow, gently turning his wrist so that he looked like he was beckoning to her.

"The police…" she began, but Grey didn't appear to be listening. Instead, his eyes were fixed on the top of the final flight of stairs above them.

There were another dozen or so of the metal steps, flattening on to another landing, this time concrete. The landing butted up against the outer wall of Brandon Mews, and a grimy glass door led into a large empty space with a domed plastic roof, encrusted with years of moss and algae. There was a lock on the door, but Izzy knew perfectly well that no resident's key fitted it.

She'd tried often enough, peering in through the dirt at the deserted corridor beyond.

Grey was frowning up at the door.

"What is it?" Izzy followed his gaze.

"Nothing... I don't know. I just thought I saw..." He blinked twice, then shook his head. "It's nothing."

Izzy moved to the bottom of the steps, all the while trying her best to ignore the shape in the water. Her best wasn't good enough. It was an effort to speak, to form the words and make them come out in the right order – to say what she was thinking. It was an effort even to think.

"We have to go. We have to find Mia, call the police. We can't just leave him here." Izzy's eyes kept sliding back to Dom. It really did look like he was watching her, waving to her. It was going to take a long time to get that particular idea out of her head. If she had been sleeping normally, it was the kind of thing she knew would turn up in her nightmares.

Except she wasn't sleeping, was she? None of them were.

Shaken, Grey leaned on the concrete balustrade of the steps. He straightened up almost immediately, paced from one side of the landing to the other and then leaned on the balustrade again. His footsteps sounded heavier than they usually did, as though he were carrying a dead weight. "You're right," he said quietly, looking at Izzy. "We should find Mia. We'll get her home and call the police from there."

Juliet let out a howl. "We can't just leave him here!"

"What do you want to do, Jools? You want to fish him out of the water? You want to carry him around the Barbican?" Grey's voice was low but angry. "Maybe we should take him home; drop him on the sofa?"

"No." She lowered her chin and shook her head, refusing to look him in the eye.

It was like being in the middle of a bad dream. Together, they turned and walked down the steps and away from the waterfall, leaving what was left of Dom still bobbing in the current. Izzy had seen him. She'd seen him. She knew it was horribly, hopelessly real … and yet somehow, she didn't quite believe it. She couldn't … couldn't bring herself to. It was Dom. Just yesterday he'd been sitting in Tigs's apartment, hadn't he? Sitting there and talking about how someone was watching them. How someone was following them.

What if there had been someone between the gates with her earlier; someone else? What if she hadn't been imagining it?

And what if, Izzy thought, her blood turning cold even as the idea crossed her mind, *the person in the garden and Dom's killer were the same...?*

Tigs opened the door to Mia's duplex when they rang the doorbell. Her eyes were red as she answered Izzy's unspoken question.

"Mia's in her room. She asked me to come over and wait in case Dom came back. I thought it was him," she said quietly. "When the door opened. I thought it was him, and everything was all right. But then she said..." Tigs stopped talking, her voice fading to nothing. She stood back to let them inside. Looking at the others, Izzy wondered whether they felt the same way she did. It was a kind of heavy numbness, like being under a huge weight of water.

At the thought of water, the image of Dom flashed before her eyes, beckoning to her. Calling her. Light flashed on flowing water, reminding her of broken glass.

As she walked through the narrow entrance hall and into the living room, she was startled to see Noah sitting at the table, a pile of paper spread out in front of him. "Where've you been?" she asked. He blinked slowly at her.

"Could ask you the same thing." He paused, and the temperature in the room dropped. Then he tapped the top sheet. "I was doing this. You all need to see it."

"Can't it wait?" Grey already had the landline handset in his palm. "We need to call the police."

"I really don't think that's a good idea, Grey." Noah's voice was flat.

"I'm sorry ... what?" Grey stared at him. So did everyone else.

Noah stared blankly at his papers. "You can't call the police."

"Again, *what*?"

"You can't call the police. Not yet, at least. I'm not sure they're going to be able to help us."

"Dom is dead, Noah. We're calling the police."

"Yeah. No." Before anyone could react, Noah had jumped up from his chair and knocked the phone out of Grey's hand. It clattered to the floor, its back cover and batteries spinning across the wood and under the sofa.

"What's the matter with you?" Izzy seemed to be the only one who could speak – Grey, Juliet and Tigs were just staring at Noah.

"Remember that video? The one of the guy who took the FokusPro?"

"The prisoner?" Grey found his voice. "The crazy guy?"

"Him. Guess what? He wasn't crazy when he took it." Noah riffled through his pile, finally settling on a sheet from somewhere in the middle. He pulled it out and slid it across the table, tapping it pointedly. "When he took it, he was one of the most decorated snipers any army's ever seen. He was hand-picked, along with another twenty or so soldiers, to test a new performance drug the military were developing for troops. It was supposed to give them an edge when they went on patrol or on missions or whatever. In the beginning, they trialled it on snipers serving in the Balkans, then on soldiers in Iraq and Afghanistan."

"And?"

"And it worked so well that they tried making it stronger. Which is when it did *that*. You can read

153

about it, if you want. It took a bit of digging, but I found out enough to make you want to throw up a couple of times. I did, anyway." He waved at the stack of paper. "What it boils down to, though, is this – twenty-five soldiers were selected for the first-in-human trials of a drug a hell of a lot like FokusPro. A couple of weeks later, almost all of them reported a range of … unexpected side effects. Another week or two? They were all dead – including our friend, Mr Psychopath. He was the last one. *Was*."

Izzy was almost too afraid to ask. Almost. "The side effects. What were they?"

"I don't think you really need me to tell you, do you?" Noah's face twisted into a ghoulish smile. "Nightmares. Memory loss. Insomnia. Hallucinations – seeing things, hearing things." He snatched up a sheet and sat back in his chair to read from it. "'Subjects displayed a rapid and complete descent into violent psychosis, with absolute failure to respond to a variety of treatments. It is our finding that this is directly and solely attributable to their participation in human trials of FPX348, and as such we cannot recommend that further development of the drug should ever be permitted.'"

"What does that mean?"

"It means," said Grey slowly, "that whatever they took, it turned them into crazies, and then they died."

"Correct!" Noah was almost laughing. "Except for one thing. It's not just the drug that *they* took. It's what *we* took, too."

Chapter Ten

Izzy went cold all over. She felt the chill start somewhere on her scalp and crawl all the way down to her feet, as though someone had poured ice water over her head. "Is this real?" she said. It was all she could manage.

"Yep." Noah nodded. "I told you I'd find out what was up with those pills."

"Would've been more helpful if you'd got round to it before any of us took them, wouldn't it?" muttered Grey.

Noah simply raised an eyebrow at him. "Really? So I don't remember you asking me if I'd been able to track any more down online, then, do I?"

"Not you as well—" Izzy began, but Grey cut her off.

"Oh, come on. Like you wouldn't have if you could," he snapped.

Izzy opened her mouth to reply, but nothing

came out. She was left opening and closing her mouth like an idiot.

"You still haven't explained why we shouldn't call the police." Compared to Juliet, who was now shaking on the sofa, Tigs looked and sounded remarkably calm. She poked at the pile of printouts, picking them up and flipping through them. "What about Dom?"

"Did anyone see what happened?"

"What do you think? Anyone here?" Tigs looked around the room. "No. And don't you think that if anyone else had seen, there'd be something? Police ... an ambulance ... *anything*?"

"Then it could have been an accident ... or it could not." Noah lowered his voice.

"Wait ... what?" Tigs stared at him, along with everyone else.

"Maybe he slipped. He was twitchy, he was paranoid. Maybe it was all just bad luck. But on the other hand, maybe Dom was right. Maybe he did see someone. We took an unlicensed drug – a top-secret experiment somebody's trying very hard to bury. Did it never occur to you that they might want it back?"

157

"And if they don't get it?" Grey cut in, "what, they bury us instead?"

"Perhaps they don't even have to do that. They just have to wait for us to drop." Noah's voice fell to little more than a whisper.

Seeing nothing but blank, frightened faces staring back at him, Noah picked through the papers for one more. He scanned it, then put it down again.

"How do I put this simply? The FokusPro, right? It messes with the way your brain works – it has to. That's what it's designed to do. But the brain's basically the most complicated machine you could imagine. And just like any machine, if you throw one bit of it out of alignment you're going to get some consequences."

"Can you just get to it?" Grey glared at him with red-rimmed eyes. "What's going to happen to us?"

"Would you listen?" Noah stifled a yawn, then shook his head. "The drug they called FPX348 – our drug – was designed to maximize short-term function and memory. It meant anyone taking it would be able to concentrate better for longer. Sound familiar?" He shuffled in his chair, not getting any answer.

Izzy wished he'd hurry up, too. She couldn't tell whether he was dragging it out for the sake of the drama, or because he needed the time to think it out for himself. Either way, she wasn't sure she was going to be able to stand it for much longer.

Eventually, he picked up again. "Somebody, somewhere up in a shiny office, figured that it might be an idea to use a pill like FPX348 longer-term. Maybe even sell it commercially."

"To students? Like us?" Tigs seemed to be keeping up with the concept better than Izzy was.

"Who the hell knows? Either way, they started to run some tests — the final results of which you saw on that video." He cleared his throat, then continued. "How much do you know about sleep?"

"I know I've not been getting enough..." Grey grumbled.

"You've been listening, clearly. You want me to break it down into words of one syllable for you?" Noah rolled his eyes. "When you're asleep, your brain processes everything it's dealt with in the day — that's why we dream. It shunts everything from short-term to long-term memory ready for the next day. Then when you hit REM sleep, it stops producing adrenaline and temporarily paralyzes you so that it can process all the bad stuff you've seen or heard without you acting it out and … I dunno, running around screaming or something."

"And that's a bad thing?" Izzy would happily admit to being nowhere near as smart as Noah. None of them were, although most of the time they didn't like to say it, not unless they could immediately turn round and say they were just kidding. But this was confusing and it was frightening, and the more he talked about sleep, the more she wanted to yawn and curl up into a little ball and just close her eyes, even if it was only for a few minutes.

"It is if you muck up the way your brain handles it all, yeah. And that's what we've done. As our murderous friend on the video discovered, you take FPX348 for more than a couple of days and your brain forgets how to shut down its adrenaline production. Any issues you have? Any trauma? Anything whatsoever that might count as having had a crap day? It sticks there, and it just kind of festers."

"What happens then?"

"What would happen if you left your lunch in the

bottom of your schoolbag? And then you did the same thing the next day?"

"Eeew."

"Exactly. Now imagine what it would be like after, ooh, say two weeks?"

Izzy's mind presented her with a mental image of her brain, stuffed full of rotten sushi and gluey-green sandwiches. Judging by the others' faces, they were thinking something pretty similar.

"So, what's the problem? None of us have taken any of the pills for ages now – have we?" Tigs shot a meaningful glance around the room.

"You would think like that, wouldn't you?" Noah didn't bother to disguise the contempt in his voice. "What happens when a cog in an engine slips?"

"Like I'm supposed to know?" Tigs pulled a face. Of course she wouldn't know, would she?

"It sends everything out of balance. And the longer it goes on, the worse it gets."

"But we're not talking about engines, are we? So isn't there something we can just, like, take?"

"No. We're not. We're talking about something a lot more complicated, which even brain surgeons don't totally understand. And you'd think they'd be pretty up on this stuff, right? That's how much trouble we're in, Tigs, seeing as you need me to spell it out. You can't fix this just by chucking another pill down your throat, all right?" As he spoke, Noah's voice climbed to a shout, and he got up from his chair and took one step at a time towards Tigs until he was almost nose-to-nose with her. She shrank back and Grey reached for Noah's arm, but Noah shook him off and glowered at him. Izzy caught the look he gave Grey – and the most frightening thing about it was that it was almost completely empty of anything or anyone she recognized. It was pure rage. There was no sign of Noah in that look – just a stranger. An *angry* stranger, who could be capable of anything.

Grey stood his ground and edged between Noah and Tigs. "Enough," he said calmly, and nodded towards the papers on the table. "You were talking about sleep, right?"

"I... Sleep? What?" Noah blinked, and suddenly he was himself again. He stepped away from Tigs, confused, and moved back to the table. "Right. Yes. Sleep. So while all this is going on in your head, your sleep cycles are out of whack and your brain just ... forgets how to do it properly."

"Which is why none of us are sleeping…"

"Bingo. Now, here's the thing – because you're not sleeping right, your brain stops producing the hormone that regulates sleep. Which means you don't sleep right, which means you don't make the hormone … and round and round we go. We've got a couple of weeks' worth of it stored in reserve, just knocking around in our systems, but once you run out … that's it. Done. Meanwhile, all the crap that goes on in the day is still getting stuffed into the brain and it's getting more and more cluttered. Think of it like a computer. If you never shut the system down, it never clears the memory, and eventually it just runs out of processing power and crashes."

"What does that mean for us?"

"Well, as far as I can make out, it means we go psycho. And then, because pretty much our entire system just packs in, we die."

"Oh."

"That's the bit where I threw up."

He handed what appeared to be a very official-looking document to Grey, who took it and started to look through the stapled pages. As he flipped, Noah said, "You have no idea how many firewalls I had to go through to find that."

"No one could trace it, though, could they? Or find you? Find us?" Grey looked up, alarmed, but Noah snorted.

"Please. You think this is my first rodeo?" His attempt at a joke felt out of place.

"This is pretty useless, you know." Grey passed the papers to Izzy. They were a mass of thick black lines, as though someone had been through huge chunks of the text with a big black marker pen. 'REDACTED' appeared in the margins in intimidating block lettering every now and again, just for variety.

"This isn't exactly helping." She gave it back to Noah, who shrugged.

"Not much does."

"So that's it. You're saying we're screwed, right?"

"Maybe."

Grey laughed. It wasn't a happy laugh. "*Maybe?* Because to me, that didn't sound like much of a maybe. It sounded pretty definite."

"There's a thing. It might work – I don't know. Not for sure."

"Right now, I'll take 'might work' over 'dead man walking'."

"I said we've all got a couple of weeks of these magic happy brain hormones, right? The ones that help keep everything on track — and which we've managed to screw up with Antigone's Marvellous Medicine? Somewhere in all this junk, I came across something about a way of kickstarting it. Something about…" He started to scatter pages across the table, the floor, the chair — skimming through them in search of the one he wanted. "That's it. Your brain's craving sleep. It needs sleep. Your brain's not prepared to go down without a fight, and it'll do anything it can to protect itself and survive. It's hardwired into it. If you can force your brain into a critically sleep-deprived state, it puts so much stress on the whole thing that it reboots the adrenal glands, the endocrine system, the whole shebang. Totally floods the brain with all the right hormones, thus saving both your sanity and your life." He wound up with a flourish.

"And you didn't lead with this … why?"

"Because."

"Because what?"

"Because you have to do it before it's too late — leave it too long and the damage can't be fixed."

"So?"

"I don't know, OK? I mean, eventually, there's always a chance the whole thing will sort itself out… But from all the stuff I've read, it's looking far more likely that by that point you'd be a monster, a vegetable or dead. Or all three."

"So it's worth a shot," said Grey.

"I'd say anything's worth a shot, wouldn't you?" Noah was deadly serious as he looked at each of them in turn.

The question they all wanted to ask came from the sofa. It was Juliet. "What do we have to do?"

"Stay awake," Noah said.

"Stay awake?" Grey repeated. "That's *it*?"

"That's it. Trigger the happy-brain hormone flood and ride the wave out all the way back to normal. Oh, and don't get killed in the meantime."

It seemed too easy, somehow. *After all*, thought Izzy, *it was just staying awake. How hard could that be?* She'd spent enough times out until the early hours, and done enough all-night study sessions to know she could do it. And after all Noah's doomy predictions about what could happen, it didn't seem difficult *enough*.

Grey spoke first. "How long? How long do we need to stay awake for?"

"Continuously? Forty-eight hours, as far as I can tell. Maybe more. It'll be different for everyone, but from what I've read, it looks like somewhere between thirty-six and forty-eight hours should do it. Basically, as long as you can. No naps. No dozing. Nothing. Stay awake till you drop. Longer if you can handle it."

"Forty-eight hours? That's a long time, Noah."

"You think?"

"It's two days. Two days, and two nights. All of them. In one go."

"Hey, you asked."

Grey sighed. "That doesn't mean I have to like the answer."

Izzy yawned – and across the room, she saw Tigs and Juliet doing exactly the same thing.

"And what about these people?" she asked. "The ones you think are after the pills … or us? Did they… Did they kill Dom?"

"Maybe. Maybe not. All I know is we can't let our guard down."

"And Dom? What about him?" Juliet interrupted.

Noah cocked his head on one side as he looked at her. "Jools? I loved Dom. I mean, I really did.

He was my best friend. Look, I don't want this to sound harsh, but he's done. We can't help him any more. Here's who we can help – you, me, Grey, Izzy, Tigs, Mia. That's who we need to worry about right now. Dom…" his voice cracked and he bit his lip. A moment later, he tried again. "If somebody did something to Dom, we'll find a way to make it right later. But now? We look after us."

"And the police? Why don't we just tell them? Tell them everything," Juliet chipped in.

There was an awkward silence. Nobody wanted to be the first to say it, but from the way the others were fidgeting, avoiding Juliet's gaze, Izzy could tell what they were thinking – and it was exactly the same thing she was. Going to the police really would mean telling them *everything*. About the pills. About where they'd got them from. What if they were illegal? What if they'd done something much, much worse than just fixing their exams? Once they told someone, anyone, there was no going back. And there would be consequences … for all of them.

It was Noah who finally spoke up. "Do you really want to sit down in an interview room and explain everything I've just told you to the police? You *really* think they'd take you seriously? Best case, they'd laugh you out of the building. Worst case … well."

"What if there are people after us? Clearing up the mess?" Grey sounded thoughtful.

"Then we'll have to deal with that, I guess." Noah started to crumple up the sheets of paper. "But for now, we stick to the plan." He strode into the kitchen, coming back out carrying a metal bin and setting it on the floor at the end of the table.

"And what is 'the plan', exactly?"

Noah swept all the crumpled paper into the bin. He pulled a lighter out of his pocket and snapped it open. A small flame wavered just above his fingers. "It's really simple. You want to survive? Stick together and *don't go to sleep*."

He dropped the lighter into the bin, and together they watched as the flames consumed the paper inside.

Chapter Eleven

"We should get Mia." Juliet was the first one to remember that she was upstairs.

"She's not asleep, is she?" Noah's voice rang with concern. It sounded like he was more worried that she might have dozed off than that she might be upset. Given what he'd just said to them all, it was a fair enough point.

"She just found her drowned brother, Noah. Do you *really* think she could sleep?" Juliet was already heading towards the stairs up to Mia's bedroom.

"What do we do about him? Dom, I mean?" Grey was looking out of the window, his fingers running up and down the edge of the slatted wooden blind that covered part of the view over the lake and gardens. Thankfully, the duplex faced the opposite end of the Barbican to the one where Dom was currently lying.

"Like I said, we can't go to the police."

"We could report him missing?"

At the bottom of the stairs, Juliet stopped. "And what happens when they actually find him? They'll want to know what happened…"

"*We* want to know what happened, don't we?" Grey slapped at the blind. It swung back and forth, tapping against the frame of the window.

Noah wasn't listening. Instead, he was running his hands back and forth through his hair, scratching at his scalp over and over again. When he finally stopped and his hands dropped back to his sides, Izzy's stomach lurched as she saw that his fingernails were red.

"How easy was it to see him?"

"You what?" Grey spun away from the window and stared at Noah in disbelief.

"How… Could anyone just … *find* him? If they weren't looking?"

"You're serious, aren't you? You're actually serious."

"Yes, I'm serious. You really think I'm mucking around?"

"I don't know what to think. None of us do, right?" Grey looked around at Izzy and Juliet for backup. Juliet just stared at her feet. Something in her had broken back at the waterfall. Izzy wondered whether it was Juliet's heart.

It felt like there wasn't enough air in the room for all of them. The light had gone from the sky, and all the warmth with it. Izzy didn't know why or how, or what it meant, but everywhere was suddenly cold and dark and she could barely breathe. Her thoughts tumbled over each other, moving too fast to hold down or to grab on to. But the one pin-sharp thing she was sure of was that Dom was dead, and if Noah was right any of them could be next. All of them could be. It was unreal.

But it *was* real. It was happening.

And the worst part was that they'd done it to themselves.

There were no monsters. There were no ghosts, no demons, no witches wishing bad things on them. No one had played truth or dare; no one had torn up a chain letter. No one had stood in front of a mirror and chanted, and no one had read so much as a single word of Latin from an old book they'd found in an abandoned cellar.

No ghosts…

"Noah?" said Izzy.

"Mmm?"

"The side effects. You said 'hallucinations'."

"Yeah, you know … seeing things, hearing things that aren't there. The usual."

"Because I think I have. I know I have. Seen things."

"Like what?"

"In the station. There was a poster…" The words clogged her throat. It felt more like her lungs were full of rags than air. "The faces on it … they changed."

"Changed, how?"

"Like they were melting. Tigs and Juliet's faces, too, and the guy in the station who asked if I was feeling OK. They just melted."

"Yeah. That's the kind of thing I was talking about."

Grey stepped away from the window, his eyes searching her face. "So that's what Tigs was talking about when she said you went loopy. Why didn't you talk to me about it? You didn't say anything."

"What, and sound like I'd *actually* gone loopy? No thanks." She stopped herself from saying any more, and looked again at Noah. "Is it … going to get worse?"

"I think that's a pretty safe bet." Noah's mouth set into a grim line.

"Forty-eight hours?"

"Give or take."

"And what about Mum?" Mia asked, appearing at the bottom of the stairs. Everything about her looked dull and hollow. "What am I supposed to tell *her*?"

"Where is she?" Noah replied. "She working?"

"When isn't she? She's in Nottingham visiting a couple of suppliers. She'll be home on Friday."

"So don't tell her anything. Don't speak to her. In fact, try not to speak to anyone. The fewer people who know about this, the better."

"Have *you* told anyone?"

"Christ, no. For a start, my mother's a nurse — how *exactly* do you think she'd take the news that I'd popped a load of unlicensed pills I'd got online? What if someone else found out and thought she knew about it? What if she lost her job? We're broke enough as it is — not like all of you."

"You know what you're asking us to do, don't you? You're asking us to lie to everyone. You're asking me to pretend I don't know that Dom is out there in the water. You're asking us to pretend that everything's going to be OK when it's not…"

"It might be, Mia. It might still be OK."

"Not for Dom, it won't. And not for me, or Mum."

"Then just think how much worse it would be for her if the same thing happened to you, too."

Mia recoiled, blinking at Noah through bloodshot eyes. "Was that a threat?"

"Come off it."

"It sounded like a threat to me." She looped her arm through Tigs's and they stood side by side, staring at the others in the room. Still silent, Juliet moved closer to them, and suddenly the group was split, with Mia, Tigs and Juliet facing Noah and Grey – with Izzy frozen between them.

"I guess I don't need to point out that you're the one who got us into this." Noah jabbed a finger towards Tigs, who shook her head.

"Well, obviously. I held you down and poured the pills down your throat, didn't I?"

"You might as well have…"

"Seriously? You know why you took them, just as well as the rest of us do. You even tried to get more. Admit it. You wanted to win."

"From where I'm standing right now, this doesn't look like winning." Grey snarled at them both, taking a swing at a pile of magazines stacked on the table.

Everyone watched as the pile slumped sideways. It probably wasn't quite the dramatic gesture Grey had been hoping for, but maybe it was better that way.

Izzy couldn't take it any more. She was so tired. Everything ached. Her mouth felt like it was full of cotton wool and a sharp, sparkling pain that had settled behind her eyes was threatening to turn into a proper headache. She pinched the bridge of her nose, hoping it would help, but all that happened was her already-tired eyes started to water. It was all too much, and she could barely hold back her yell of frustration. Noah was sniping at Tigs. Mia was angry, Grey was angry. Juliet was a mess and…

Everything became very clear again in an instant, as Izzy's gaze locked on to the open front door behind Mia and Tigs, and the empty space where Juliet had been standing a moment before.

"Guys…? Where did Juliet go?"

It had got surprisingly late. Outside, the sky was darkening to a velvety blue. Mia slammed the door behind them. "Where would she go?"

"I don't know." Izzy already had her phone in her

hand and was dialling Juliet's number. It rang once, then cut out as they passed behind the shadow of Lauderdale Tower and the signal vanished. "Stupid phone…" She swore at it and tried again, but it stubbornly refused to connect. By now, they were on the walkway over the middle of the lake again – and every single one of them was completely fixed on not looking over their shoulder towards the waterfall. It wasn't that Dom was suddenly any less important. It was simply that there wasn't much any of them could do to help him. There would be time for Dom. It just wasn't now.

"Come on!" Grey was ahead, hurrying them on. "How long ago did she leave? Did anyone see her? Noah? Iz?"

"I didn't. I wasn't looking. It must have been when Grey knocked the magazines over. We were all watching him, weren't we? I mean, after everything I said about sticking together I wasn't exactly expecting her to just … run off!" Noah sounded slightly out of breath. He was clearly struggling against exhaustion. Izzy knew how *that* felt – every step was like trying to run through syrup. Forty-eight hours suddenly seemed like a very long time.

They reached the end of the bridge, and ahead of them the long curving walkway swept around the back of the Barbican Centre. Izzy eyed it, thinking of the phantom footsteps she'd heard there. Had that been yesterday or today? And the lift – the horrible, horrible lift. Was that only this morning? It seemed so much longer ago than that. Everything was distorting, twisting – just like the faces on that poster. Knowing it was all in her head should make her feel better, she knew that, but somehow, it didn't. Somehow, it made her feel worse. Because no matter where she went or what she did, there was no escape. Nowhere to run or to hide. The horror went with her.

Forty-eight hours suddenly seemed like a very, *very* long time indeed.

They ran down the ramp from the bridge to the entrance level of the Barbican Centre, barging through groups of theatregoers there for the evening show.

"Sorry, sorry, sorry…" Grey muttered as they shouldered their way through the crowd and out of the doors on to the lakeside terrace. The globe-shaped lighting cast strange shadows on the paving and on the concrete walls of the Centre, and as they ground to a halt to catch their breath and to look around, Izzy could have sworn she saw one of the shadows move.

"Have you got her yet?" Tigs peered over Izzy's shoulder at her phone.

"Not yet…" She dialled again and, this time, the phone rang. "Call Kara. Juliet might have gone to her place…"

"*I'm* not calling Kara," Tigs snorted.

Mia shook her head. "Now, Tigs? You're going to be like this now? *God.* I'll call her. We need to find Juliet…" She tailed off, and took out her own phone.

"Before it's too late." Noah finished the sentence for her and hopped on to one of the outdoor tables nearby, picking his way between a couple of empty beer bottles and wine glasses as he scanned the terrace for any sign of Juliet. "I don't think she's here."

On the other end of Izzy's phone line, there was a muffled scrabbling sound, and then a quiet, "Hello?"

"Juliet!" Izzy stuck her hand in the air and flapped it to get the others' attention. They crowded around her — all except for Mia, who was speaking quickly into her own phone. She must have got hold of Kara.

"Jools, where are you? We're coming to get you."

"I can't. I just … can't. I'm sorry, OK? I can't pretend and I can't lie about it. I have to tell someone. I have to. Dom. He's… I'm sorry… But my parents. Maybe they can help…" She was out of breath, and in the background Izzy could hear car horns, a siren.

A moment later, the same siren passed somewhere nearby.

"Jools, where are you? It's not safe."

"I'm sorry…" Juliet whispered again, and the line went dead.

Izzy stared at her phone, then looked at the others. "She hung up."

Noah jumped down from the table. "We have to find her. Did she say where she was?"

"No, but she's not far. She's on the street. That siren that just went along the road? It went past her first."

Grey cut in. "It was an ambulance, wasn't it?" He frowned. "She's in Smithfield. She's heading for Bart's."

"The hospital?"

"Her parents, remember?"

Izzy went cold. Juliet's mum and dad were both

doctors at St Bartholomew's Hospital, right around the corner.

She was going to tell them everything.

"There's only two ways she could have gone – either down Long Lane, or down Carthusian Street," said Grey, as they hurried up a flight of steps towards the nearest exit from the Barbican's walls. "If we split into two groups and each take one of those, we should meet at Smithfield Market and be able to catch her before she makes it to the main entrance of Bart's."

In her mind, Izzy could picture Juliet making her way down one of those two roads, pushing through crowds of commuters heading to the Tube station, past the pubs and the sandwich shops – now closed for the day, their blinds pulled down – towards the Victorian hulk of Smithfield meat market, squatting in the centre of the district. By now, the market would be starting to come to life, the refrigerated lorries all beginning to arrive as the butchers' stalls opened up ready for another night of trading. It had surprised Izzy, when they had first moved to the Barbican, that the market only opened at night.

Walking through it one day, she'd asked Grey why, and he had laughed. "Vampires, innit?" he'd said with a shrug. The truth was that, like most of the big London markets, it opened at night so all the restaurants could get their supplies for the next day's meals, but for a while, the sound of the lorries arriving through the night had made her smile to herself.

They decided that Mia and Noah would go ahead on Long Lane, which ran straight from the Barbican to the entrance to Bart's Hospital. Izzy, Grey and Tigs would head down Carthusian Street, running parallel to Long Lane. On the way, Tigs would collect Kara from her building just around the corner, and the two of them would separate off and check the back of Charterhouse Square, with its private garden, just to be sure, and then hang back in case Juliet changed her mind and backtracked. There was no way they could miss her.

"Nobody's on their own, everybody stays safe," said Noah.

"You really do think there's someone after us, don't you?" Mia said quietly, rubbing her fingers along the hem of her top.

"I don't know what to think." Noah shrugged. "But better safe than sorry, right?"

They crossed the busy main road below the wall marking one of the Barbican's boundaries and stopped outside the Tube station. Izzy watched as Noah and Mia disappeared round the corner and down Long Lane, then turned to follow Tigs and Grey in the opposite direction, up the road towards Carthusian Street. Had Juliet come this way? What was she thinking? What if Dom had been right? What if Noah was right? What if there really was someone watching them … following them?

And worse, what if Juliet really did tell her parents about the pills? What then?

The world spun around her and suddenly she couldn't see Grey or Tigs. They had been there a second ago, right by the postbox. But everything seemed to have skipped ahead. Again, it was like she was watching a film that glitched. She had blinked, and everything had shifted forward.

"Oh, no…"

The streetlight overhead flickered, then fizzled out with a smell of smoke.

"It's not real. It's not real."

But it felt real. The shiver that ran down her spine felt real. The hairs standing up on her arms felt real. The prickling along her scalp, beneath her hair – that felt real, too. The cool of the wall that she backed herself into? Real. The interesting smell coming from the guy in the battered green parka and filthy jeans who just brushed past her to get to the cash machine? Very real.

Maybe that was the trick? If you knew it wasn't real, it wasn't so bad. Maybe you could stop it. Maybe that was the way...

The man in the parka stopped dead. And then slowly, so slowly, he began to turn towards her, almost like he was on a turntable. His feet didn't move, and neither did his legs or his head. He just *revolved* until he was facing her. Dirty blond hair fell across his face, hiding it, and the way it was all matted together, it couldn't have been washed in months.

Izzy squeezed her eyes shut. "Don't look. Not real. Don't look. Not real..." she whispered to herself over and over again. Sure enough, nothing happened. Nobody seemed to notice. No one stopped to say anything to her. Everything was *normal*. She was just a girl standing at the side of the street, leaning against the stone front of a bank. Maybe she was waiting for a bus. With her eyes shut.

It was all in her head. And if it was all in her head, she could make it go away. It was *her* head, wasn't it? And if it was her head, that made it her story. Her rules.

She took a deep breath. She had to open her eyes; had to catch up with the others. Maybe Grey was already coming back for her.

She opened one eye, keeping her gaze firmly fixed on a lump of chewing gum beside her foot. It was fine. The world was fine. It was all in her head.

She opened the other eye and looked up.

He was waiting.

As she raised her head, the man in the parka was in her face – barely a finger-length from her. He leaned close, stretching his neck further than anyone should have been able to. He reeked of decay, of something old and rotten, and when he opened his mouth, his teeth were blackened stumps that made her think of logs left after a fire. His hair still hung over his face, but as he leaned in and let out a shriek that grated along her bones, it blew back and away from his face.

He had no eyes.

There were only bloody sockets where his eyes should have been, and as he shrieked and she screamed, he raised his hand almost to her face. His fingers and nails were twisted like claws, and Izzy couldn't tell where the nail ended and the finger began. She could almost feel them brush against her – nails sharp as knives, and flesh unpleasantly soft and wet against her skin – when he snapped his arm back. His lower jaw twisted into something that could have been a grin, and then he dug his nails deep into the flesh of his forehead. Dark, sticky liquid oozed out as he began to tear off his own face in front of her.

She couldn't scream any more. Couldn't even move. All she could do was watch as flesh peeled away from bone, as black blood bubbled up around his fingertips and dripped down the stranger's, the … *thing's* face. It couldn't be a man. What kind of man could do that?

Ribbons of skin flopped wetly around her feet, and still he tore and still he made that awful sound. And she was sure that somehow, from behind his missing eyes, he was watching her. Watching her fear. Watching her and enjoying it…

"Izzy!"

She heard her name, and jerked her head sideways. The world skipped again, jumped back into step.

"You're OK. You're OK." Grey had his hand on her arm.

The stranger was gone.

There was no blood on the pavement, no strips of flesh and skin. Just a pinkish-grey sucker of chewing gum.

He wasn't real.

She knew he wasn't real, even as Grey pulled her away from the wall and put an arm around her and she felt her whole body trembling with fright against him.

He wasn't real. He wasn't real. He wasn't real. He couldn't have been real. Couldn't have been.

If she kept telling herself that, maybe after a while she would start to believe it.

Chapter Twelve

"Are we going to have a problem?" Grey asked, pulling away from her gently.

"No, I'm fine. I am. It was just..." Izzy stared up into his eyes. "It was so real."

"You want to tell me about it?"

"No!" It came out as a shout. "No, I just want to forget it," she said, more softly.

"I didn't mean it to make you feel better," he said with a shrug. "I mean, I want to know what's coming."

"You've not seen anything yet?"

"Maybe. I think... I mean... How would I know if I had? Dom didn't seem to be able to tell the difference..."

"Oh, you'd know," Izzy said, her voice grim.

Tigs was standing on the corner, waiting for them. "Are you done with your little drama, then?" she asked, but she looked uncomfortable and she kept shifting her feet as though there was something on the ground she was trying to avoid. Izzy looked her up and down and, despite herself, she smiled.

"It's started, hasn't it?"

"Huh?" Tigs blinked at her and for a second, Izzy saw underneath the usual Tigs façade. She looked exhausted and, more than that, she looked scared. Her eyes looked like they had been forced wide open and held that way with pins, and her whole body was tense.

"You've seen something."

"Rats," Tigs said with a shudder. "There were rats. Not, like, normal rats. Not like that at all. They had ... teeth, and ... eyes ... and ... everyone was staring but nobody ... nobody..." She gulped. "They were everywhere. And they were... They were..." She shivered, unable to finish even part of the story. A little voice at the back of Izzy's head said that Tigs had no idea how lucky she was only to be seeing rats. Even if they did have teeth and eyes. Especially if they had teeth and eyes, come to think of it, because surely rats without either of those would be worse?

"There's no rats," Grey said, although he glanced

around on the pavement, just to be sure. "And we've got to go."

Right on cue, Tigs's phone beeped and the softer, scared Tigs disappeared. The old Tigs was back. "Kara." She glared at the message on her screen. "She's waiting. Like it's not bad enough that we're probably all going to die. I have to die with *Kara*."

"Jesus, Tigs. Of all the things to be freaked by. What's your problem with her now? Especially if she helps keep you alive?" Grey asked over his shoulder. He was already striding ahead down Carthusian Street.

"Nothing," Tigs snapped back, but Grey didn't seem to hear.

"You're not OK, are you? Not really," Izzy said gently, and Tigs's shoulders slumped.

"No. I'm not." She stopped walking and looked at Izzy, who realized that Tigs's eyes were full of tears. "I'm so sorry, Izzy. I'm sorry about the pills. I didn't know. You have to believe me…"

"Of course I do."

"They were supposed to help. They were supposed to help *all* of us – Kara, too. So we could be sure nobody had to leave and we could all stay together.

I had no idea… And Dom … and…" She looked like she was about to break down. "I didn't know. I didn't. I didn't."

"I believe you, Tigs. None of us knew."

"You don't blame me? Not like Noah?"

"Noah's just scared. We all are. Nobody blames you. Not really." Izzy hadn't even finished speaking before she wondered whether that was a lie.

Kara was waiting for them on the steps outside the Art Deco front of Florin Court. It was a shock to see her again. She looked so normal. So ordinary. Her eyes weren't red and sore and there were no dark shadows below them. There was no sign of the greyish pallor that the rest of them had. Kara's skin as good as glowed.

"You look awful! All of you." Kara was clearly as shocked by the way they looked as they were by her.

"Thanks," Tigs shot back, her vulnerability vanishing in a heartbeat.

Grey tipped his head on one side. "Are you going to play nice?" he asked Tigs, who rolled her eyes.

"I'm fine. Just go, all right? And … be careful. I mean it." There was something in her voice that wasn't usually there. A warmth. Concern. Her gaze flickered from Grey to Izzy. "Seriously. *Be careful.*"

They didn't need telling twice.

"Do you think they've found her?" Izzy was breathless from keeping up with Grey, even though he was obviously struggling, too. His path was no longer straight, and when they had to step into the road to pass the hoarding around the borehole for a new Underground tunnel, he came dangerously close to walking straight in front of an oncoming taxi. The cab's horn blared as, headlights flashing, it swerved and Izzy yanked Grey back on to the safety of the pavement.

Grey scratched his head. "Whoops."

"Yeah. Whoops." She nodded towards the roof of the market ahead of them. "We cut through the middle, right?"

The main building of Smithfield meat market was, unlike most markets, divided in two by an open-ended central aisle – a semi-pedestrianized road running through the middle. It was a busy commercial market, where forklifts laden with crates and carcasses buzzed up and down the aisle all night. But for now, it was still quiet. Access to the refrigerated stalls themselves was through two large gates that opened off the aisle, or directly through the loading docks – a setup designed to keep the stalls as clean and cool as possible. Several of the loading bays had lorries parked outside them already but Grey and Izzy raced past, down as far as the path through the centre of the market.

Izzy pulled her phone out of her pocket as they went and stared at it. Nothing. There was still no sign of Juliet, and no word from Noah.

On the other side of the market, the road opened out into the large circular space of West Smithfield. Trees and cobblestones surrounded a ramp that swept down to an underground car park, and right in front of them was one of the entrances to the hospital – a grand gateway cut into a high stone wall. Through it, a courtyard with a huge fountain in the middle was just visible.

There was nobody there. So where were Juliet, Noah and Mia?

"Plan?" Izzy sank on to a bench beside the car park ramp.

"Go in?" Grey flopped on to the seat next to her. "They must all be inside."

"You think they went in after her?"

"I don't think anything any more. I tap out when I get past 'Need to sleep'."

"And that's how you're keeping going, is it? Not thinking?"

"Usually." He winked at her and stood up, but she could tell even he had less energy than he normally did. The Grey she knew, the one who was always joking and messing about, was slipping away. Was that what was happening to her, too? It sure felt like it. It felt like everything that should be her, everything that she normally was, was asleep somewhere… And instead, there was a washed-out version of her walking around. A dream version.

Not for the first time, Izzy found herself wondering whether all this was just a dream. A bad dream brought on by too much pressure at school, and tomorrow she'd wake up and it would be the last day of term and she'd never have taken the pills. And she never would. She pinched herself experimentally. It hurt.

"Did you just do what I think you did?" Grey was leaning away from her, staring at her like she'd just grown another head.

"No," she scoffed, then shuffled on the bench. "Maybe... Stop judging me, all right?"

Grey didn't reply. Instead, he stared at the main gate into Bart's Hospital.

Guessing what he was thinking, Izzy hauled herself up off the bench. "Come on, then."

"You want to go in?"

"Well, we can't exactly sit here all night, can we?"

"It's one way to kill the time."

"Can we not use that word?"

"What word?"

"You know. 'Kill'." She dropped her voice to a whisper.

He paused, trying to work out how serious she was being. And then, at long last, he cracked a grin. "Loser," he whispered back.

It was only for a second. But just for that one second they were normal again, themselves again. And it was enough to keep her going.

The receptionist was not happy about letting them in. Izzy couldn't blame her. She probably thought they were there to case the joint and raid the pharmacy. Izzy had caught sight of her own reflection in the glass of the door as they'd walked in, and it was fair to say that if she'd been the receptionist, she wouldn't have let them in, either. Her hair looked like someone had dropped a damp, dark, tangled mop on her head from a great height. Her eyes were red (no surprise there) and her skin had turned a sort of pale greeny-blue. The shadows under her eyes had darkened so much they looked like someone had punched her, and her lips were starting to chap and crack.

"We look like a couple of junkies," she whispered to Grey as he sidled up to the front desk.

"The irony of that is not lost on me, you know," he whispered back, before turning what he clearly meant to be a dazzling smile at the woman on the other side of the desk.

It had been *intended* as a dazzling smile. It fell quite a long way short.

The receptionist took one look at the pair of them and pointed at a row of chairs pushed back against the opposite wall. "Wait there." She glared at them and was about to pick up the handset of the phone that sat in front of her when another member of staff appeared, clutching a pile of folders. The receptionist glared at them both again, then turned her attention to her colleague.

"Now," Grey hissed at Izzy. "Juliet's parents share an office on the fifth floor."

"An office?"

"Look, I don't know how that works. I just know they have one, I've been in there. Fifth floor, out the lift, turn right. Then just follow the signs to the department that has too many vowels in it." He glanced over at the desk. "Before she remembers we're here, OK? Juliet must be up there somewhere. Look for her in the corridor, then come straight back down. I'll meet you on the other side of the entrance."

"I thought we weren't supposed to split up?" Izzy stood up and stretched, inching towards the lifts as casually as she could. She could feel her spine clicking. Feel every bone in her shoulders and arms complaining.

"If we both try and get in that lift, she'll have Security down here in an instant. You're in a public place…"

"Like the Barbican?" she said pointedly.

Grey frowned. "I know, but it's different, isn't it? Go, look, come back. If you're not back in ten minutes, I'm coming in after you. And God help you if you've stopped to put on lippy or something."

"Are you serious?" Izzy shot him a disbelieving look, but then the lift pinged and the doors clattered open. Seizing her chance, she slipped inside and pressed the button for the fifth floor.

The lift did not go up. The lift went down.

Izzy tried pressing the button for the fifth floor again, but the controls ignored her and the lift rattled towards the basement. There was nothing to do but go along for the ride. "I must have really bad lift-juju," Izzy muttered as the doors opened again and released her. She peered out into the corridor, stepping gingerly through the doors.

"Oh, no…"

Izzy wasn't sure what she was looking at, but she was fairly certain that this was not what the basement of St Bartholomew's Hospital usually looked like. It was dark, for a start – a long, dark corridor lit only by the occasional bare bulb hanging from the ceiling. The paint (a sort of vomit-orange) was peeling away from the walls in big flakes, leaving mould-blackened plaster visible below. Thick pipes, encrusted with dirt and rust, were bolted to one of the walls just above head height and disappeared into the gloom. There was an overpowering smell of rot and decay, and a thickness in the air that caught in the back of her throat and made her gag.

"Nope. Not again…" She spun back towards the lift, but the doors had somehow closed without her hearing them and the lift was gone. She pressed the 'call' button over and over again, but there was no telltale whir from inside the lift shaft.

She was stuck, and there was nothing to do but try and ride it out.

From somewhere in the dark of the corridor, there came a squeaking sound. Just once. Then nothing.

Then it came again. And again, and again.

It was a wheel, squeaking.

Something was coming toward her, down the corridor.

"OK, Iz. OK. You're OK. It's all in your head. It can't hurt you. Nothing in your head can hurt you.

Just go with it," Izzy muttered under her breath, already feeling her pulse rising.

The squeaking got louder. Closer.

Something was moving along the corridor, slowly and evenly. She could make out the movement now as whatever it was passed through each of the pools of light in turn.

Closer and closer.

Squeak. Squeak. Squeak.

And something else. Something quieter. A kind of rattle, like metal on metal.

Izzy breathed deeply, slowly, and coughed at the taste of the air. It was like breathing moss.

Creak–rattle. Creak–rattle. Creak–rattle.

Someone was humming.

It was a woman – and now, Izzy could see her. It was a nurse pushing a metal instrument trolley, and she was coming down the corridor.

At least, she *had* been a nurse … once.

The closer she got, the more obvious it was. Her uniform was old-fashioned, like the pictures in a history textbook. She had a complicated hat made out of stiffened fabric, which looked like a piece of origami. It had a red cross on the front of it. Except the cross hadn't been painted in ink. It was painted in blood.

The edges of her uniform were tattered, torn and stained with green and brown. Her hair, escaping from beneath the edges of her hat, had been curled and pinned, but was now a dirty shade of blonde and hung limply across her face. Her lips were blood-red, but her lipstick had smeared across her cheeks, making it look as though her face had been torn open. Izzy forced herself to look away, but not before she had seen the eyes, rolled far back into her head, only the whites visible, yellowed and dirtied with age.

She'd managed to stop herself looking at the nurse, but there was still the trolley. The closer it came, the harder it was not to look. Not to see the surgical tools that had been neatly arranged on the top of it, not to see the rust that caked the edges of scissors and saws and surgical shears.

The rust, and other things.

Impossible not to see the blunt pliers at the near end of the trolley.

Impossible to miss the tray of fingernails beside them.

The squeaking stopped. The humming did not. The nurse had stopped beside a door a little way in front of her. An arrow painted on the wall beside it said 'Morgue'.

Izzy's hand crept behind her back and she pressed her thumb into the button for the lift until she thought it might snap. The nurse looked at her, and blinked her white eyes.

"You shouldn't be here, dearie," she said, and her voice sounded like it was coming from somewhere deep underground. It was muffled and thick and clogged with earth. She stepped around the trolley. "You can't be here." The nurse lifted her hand and tucked her hair behind her ear. "You can't be here," she said again, and her hand dropped to the trolley. Her mottled fingers settled on something that shone dully as she picked it up.

"I was just leaving," Izzy said as calmly as she could. She jabbed the button again as the nurse took another step closer.

It was a scalpel. Izzy could see it now; see the tip of her finger sliding up and down the back of the blade.

"I'm just waiting for the lift and then I'll be gone. I was trying to get to the fifth floor – I got kind of lost…" She hoped she sounded friendly. She also hoped that sounding friendly worked on psychotic hallucinations.

"Oh, we're all lost down here, dearie." The whisper came in Izzy's ear, and suddenly the nurse was there beside her and raising the scalpel. Izzy jerked back, but the nurse's other hand snapped forward and grabbed hold of her wrist, clamping so tightly around it that Izzy could feel her fingers throb. She tried to pull away but it was no use. She twisted, she pulled and she tugged her whole arm back, but nothing could break the nurse's grip. All she could do was watch as the empty white eyes bored into her and the nurse raised the hand that held the scalpel.

"I'm sorry," Izzy whispered, and just for a second, the monstrous nurse hesitated.

Her body aching with effort, Izzy pulled away once more. And this time, it *was* enough. The grip slipped from around her wrist and she tumbled free. The nurse lunged towards her, aiming for her face and slicing down with the scalpel. There was a pressure on her cheek, a sensation of cold and then of heat. And then the world jerked as though someone had changed the channel on a remote control and Izzy found herself sitting on the floor of the lift with the doors closing on a (thankfully empty) brightly lit, white-painted basement corridor.

All thoughts of the fifth floor, of Juliet, of anything forgotten, Izzy counted the seconds until the door opened on to the reception area. Ignoring the receptionist's shouted, "Hey!" she shouldered open the door to the outside world. Grey was there, waiting. He turned to face her and then rushed to her side.

"What happened?"

"The basement. There was…"

"Iz, why were you in the basement? I told you to go to the fifth floor."

"I tried. I did. Lift wouldn't let me." It sounded weak, however true it was. Something told her he wasn't really listening.

"Your face – what happened?" Gently, he turned her cheek toward him. "You're bleeding…" He stopped and stepped away. "And what the hell are you doing with that?"

Izzy followed his gaze down to her right hand.

She was holding a scalpel, the blade tinted red with her own blood.

Chapter Thirteen

The scalpel clattered to the ground.

There was something new in the way that Grey looked at her. Izzy could see it. Something that had not been there before.

Fear.

"I don't know where that came from…" she began, but even as she said it, she knew it was no good.

"Izzy, why were you carrying a scalpel?" He took another step back from her, putting as much space between them as he could.

"I told you, I don't know. I don't even remember…" But that wasn't quite true, was it? Images flickered through her mind. The nurse. The trolley. The corridor. And then the corridor again, but as it should have looked; as it really looked. White-painted walls and pale yellow plastic floor tiles, still damp from being mopped. A neat sign pointing to the MRI suite. A delivery man. A pile of boxes. Plastic wrapping fluttering to the floor. An open storage cupboard.

Broken glass glittering in the light and a door slamming shut.

Izzy's mouth opened and closed silently as the truth sank in. Whatever she had seen, or thought she'd seen, wasn't real. But any memory of what she might actually have done had disappeared.

"I don't remember," she said again. She had stolen a scalpel from a hospital. She had carried it back outside with her. She had come to find Grey with it still in her hand. And she had no idea how or why she had done it. "Grey? I'm scared."

"Me, too." He stepped closer again, cautiously, and poked the scalpel with the toe of his trainer. The metal blade *tinged* against the stone paving as the knife rolled over.

"I don't think it's safe here."

"I'm with you on that one." He nodded towards the gate. "Juliet's not here. We should get back to the Barbican."

"You think we're any safer there? After what happened to Dom?"

"Thing is, we don't *know* what happened to Dom, do we?" He eyed the scalpel, now lying at their feet.

"And until we do, we stick to wherever feels safest. That's –" he glanced up at the hospital building looming over them – "not here." Reluctantly, he bent to pick the scalpel up, wrapping it in a tissue and sliding it into the back pocket of his jeans. "We can't just leave it there, can we? Anything could happen to it."

"Are you sure that's a good idea?"

"Any other day? No. Today? I'm not sure."

He was right. Nothing about this made sense, and everything was wrong. But the frightening thing was that it had made sense at the time. Or at least, it had *seemed* to. Just like it had made sense to try and stop Juliet from telling her parents about the pills.

Juliet was right. Of course she was.

Juliet who was somewhere, alone.

Izzy's phone chirped, startling them both, and in her hurry to get it out of her pocket, she fumbled it, dropping it heavily on the ground. Noah's name flashed up on the screen as she scooped it back up. Noah didn't wait for her to say hello. By the time she'd got the phone to her ear, he was already talking.

"…following me. I lost Mia. I don't know where she is. We were by the market…"

"Noah, slow down. We're right across the road. Where are you?"

"I told you, I lost her. I can't find her. One minute she was behind me, and the next she was gone. And there's this *sound*. It's like… It's like there's someone whispering in my ear, all the time. I can't get away from it."

"It's in your head, Noah. Just like you said – it's not real. You've got to ignore it. We're coming to you right now. Where are you?" Izzy asked him again. She could hear him breathing heavily into his phone. He sounded panicky and he wasn't listening to anything she said. This wasn't the calm and serious Noah they all knew, not now. This was a different version of him – one who was unravelling fast.

"I think there's someone following me. I can't… I don't know. I just…" His words faded in and out as if he was turning his head away from the phone and then back again. Like he was looking around quickly, trying to spot someone in a crowd.

"Noah! Listen to me – stop. Wherever you are, just stop. We're coming to you. You just need to tell us *where you are*."

There was a crackle on the other end of the line,

and then Noah's voice again, clearer than it had been. "North side of the market…" The line went dead.

They dodged between two delivery vans and crossed the road back over to the long, single-storey structure of Smithfield's market building. With the evening light gone, the bulbs around the building had turned on, casting uneven shadows on the red bricks and the elaborate wrought-iron that decorated the edges of the roof. It looked more like a theatre than a market. A nearby lorry's air brakes hissed loudly as the two of them hurried into the central aisle of the building, doubling back the way they'd come.

The iron railings and gates dividing the market were painted in garish shades of blue and green and purple, clashing horribly in the artificial light with the bright red phone box standing in front of them. The railings separated the working areas of the market, with their refrigerated stalls, from the aisle and anyone who happened to be passing through. And while the lights were on outside the market and in the roof over the aisle, the main lights inside were still very definitely off. Tiny red and green lights glowed in the darkness of the hall – the power lights on the fridges and freezers of the stalls. The air was cooling quickly, too. It spilled through the railings and pooled around their feet. Izzy shivered. One of the market porters strode past the end of the building, whistling. In his white coat and hardhat, he was already dressed for work. There were more lorries outside, and on the street Izzy could hear the sound of loading-bay doors rolling open, of vehicles reversing into their docks and of vans hooting to get past. But although the market hall was still dark, she was sure she could hear a faint noise from within.

"Aren't we forgetting something? Like … Noah?" Grey stood beside her as she stared into the gloom.

"What if he's in there?"

"What would he be doing in there, in the dark?"

"Hiding."

"From what?"

"Everything. He was scared, Grey. *Really* scared."

Izzy leaned her head against the gate and listened. There was definitely something – it sounded like heavy plastic rustling, shifting in a breeze. She strained her ears for it, but it was almost too faint to make out.

Someone, somewhere in the darkened hall, moaned.

Izzy saw Grey's head whip round to follow the sound. "You heard that?"

"I did. You?"

"Yes."

"And that means…"

"It must be real."

There was a thick chain with a heavy padlock wrapped around the two halves of the gate into the market hall, but the padlock hung open and useless. It looked like it had been smashed open rather than just unlocked. Izzy put her shoulder against the wrought iron and pushed. The gate resisted, then swung open. Side by side, they stepped through and into the shadows of the hall. It smelled of disinfectant and raw meat. The smell hung in the air and clung to her clothes.

"Guys?" Izzy called. "Mia? Jools?"

"Noah?" Grey joined in. Their voices echoed back to them, distorted.

"Come on." Izzy pulled at Grey's arm, urging him to follow her further into the darkened market.

"You know," he whispered, taking a careful step forward, "you had no memory of taking a scalpel from Bart's. I'm not sure how I feel about the idea of you around a load of butchers' cleavers."

"Shh."

They crept forward again, still listening. Izzy could just make out the crackling, crinkling sound of plastic, right on the edge of her hearing. Grey was twitchy and wired, seeing things in every shadow, or imagining something behind every refrigerator. Maybe he really was seeing things, she thought, trying to shrug off the memory of the things she'd *already* seen.

"Any minute, someone's going to come in here and switch the lights on, and we're not supposed to be here," Grey hissed.

You shouldn't be here, dearie… The nurse's words echoed in Izzy's head.

"I know I heard something. So did you. What if it's Mia? Or Juliet? Or Noah? What if they're hurt?"

"What if we're crazy and you lose it and go after me with a knife?"

"Well, you've always said we should go on a date…"

They had almost reached the end of the hall and

they had found precisely nothing. Just a load of deserted butchers' stalls. She leaned forward to peer around the last of them. Everything was dark and quiet and still. Everything was – as far as she could tell – just the way it should be. The counter of the final stall was draped in plastic, presumably to keep it clean during the day. It swept down and over the front of the glass and almost to the floor. A draught from the refrigeration unit made it sway backwards and forward, brushing the steel of the base. That was what she'd been able to hear. She sighed with relief.

"I'll be honest, this wasn't *exactly* what I had in mind when I said that." Grey had already turned and was heading back to the gate. "But if you're—"

He stopped as, with the click of a timer and a loud buzz, the lights flicked on.

They both saw her at exactly the same time.

Above them, the roof soared upwards, supported by iron buttresses like the inside of a cathedral. And hanging from a meat hook in the middle of it was Juliet.

She had been hoisted up by a steel cable slung through the buttress and wrapped around the handle of a freezer unit. The wire had been wrapped round and round her neck before the hook had been buried in it, cutting into her throat and splaying it open. Her T-shirt and shorts were stained with the blood that had run down her body, dripping off the toe of her leopard print ballet pump as she swayed in the refrigerated air. Her pendant had fallen to the ground. The red glass had smashed into hundreds of tiny fragments, most of them lost in the pool of blood collecting below her body.

Izzy's breath caught in her throat and stuck there. Something was threatening to bubble up and out of her, but she didn't know what. For a moment it felt like laughter.

"We're going to die. We're going to die. We're going to die…" Her voice was rising and she had no way of stopping it. She couldn't stop it. All she could see was Juliet twisting above them. "We're going to die, Grey. We're going to … to—"

Grey pressed a finger to her lips. "I don't care what Noah said about Dom." Grey's voice was little more than a croak. "There's no way this was an accident."

"Noah…" Izzy repeated, tearing her gaze away from Juliet's lifeless body. Her eyes were still open and her glasses sat crookedly across the bridge of her nose. "Noah. He said…"

"He said someone was following him." Grey already knew what she was thinking. "What if they were following Juliet first?"

"I'm calling him. Now." Her hands were shaking so violently that she missed the redial button the first time she tried to hit it, and her phone let out a squawk of protest. She tried again, getting it right the second time. It rang, and rang, and rang. There was no answer.

"We have to go. Juliet's not going to stay hidden. Someone'll find her, and soon. We don't want to be here when that happens." Grey grabbed her hand and pulled her towards the exit.

"What if she's not…?"

"Look at her, Izzy. She is. Trust me. We have to leave."

Clinging to each other like their lives depended on it, they stumbled through the darkness. Only once they were out of the building did Izzy slow her pace to check her phone.

"Noah's still not answering."

"Let's just get back to the Barbican. Either your place or mine. We go in, we lock the door, we don't come out till this is over."

"He's not *answering*, Grey!"

She realized that neither of them was listening to the other. They had left Mia and Juliet. They had as good as abandoned Tigs and Kara, all thoughts of them forgotten until that moment. And wherever Noah was, he wasn't picking up – that couldn't be good.

Music spilled out of a bar on the far side of the street and there was laughter as a group of friends stood around outside, sipping drinks. They were maybe two, three years older than her at most. That was supposed to be her life.

"Try him one more time. And then we're done." They were past the market now, back on Carthusian Street, where she'd had to pull Grey out of the path of the taxi. At the end of the street, the solid concrete of the Barbican really did look like a fortress. Now, though, it wasn't intimidating. Now, it was almost welcoming. It was solid and it was safe. It had doors and locks and gates and keys.

And none of those had kept Dom safe, whispered a

voice inside her head. *Tick tock, tick tock. Stick together and stay alive.*

She fought back a sudden urge to giggle, horrified at herself. It wasn't funny. Nothing about this nightmare was funny.

And yet...

Her fingers moved of their own accord, tracing the tender streak on her cheek where the scalpel had slashed it.

When she finally realized Grey was talking to her, it was an effort to focus on his voice. She could barely make out the words.

"Are you going to call him?"

"Call who?"

"Noah, Izzy."

"Oh. Noah."

Her fingers felt as though someone had wrapped them in cotton wool. They were thick and clumsy as she fumbled with her phone.

She dialled.

And somewhere very, very close by, a mobile phone began to ring.

Izzy felt a prickle of fear down her spine. A glance at Grey told her he felt exactly the same. Tiny beads of sweat were forming on his forehead.

"Hang up," he said quietly. She did.

The phone stopped ringing.

"Now try again?"

She dialled. The call connected, and the phantom phone started to ring again.

It was coming from somewhere behind the blue painted chipboard hoarding that protected the building site in the corner of Charterhouse Square.

"Maybe he dropped his phone…" Izzy tried. Grey's face was grim.

"I think we both know that's not what happened here."

He turned towards the hoarding and ran his hands over it, testing it. It didn't give beneath the pressure of his fingers; didn't even wobble.

Finally, he dropped his hands. "We should go."

"And Noah?"

Grey didn't answer.

Izzy hadn't expected him to.

Chapter Fourteen

Neither of them spoke on the way back to Izzy's apartment, and it wasn't until they were safely in her hallway that she felt like she was actually able to talk at all. Whether or not she wanted to was a different story. She blinked, and the image of Juliet swinging from the rafters flashed in front of her, vanishing as she opened her eyes. She blinked again, and there was the body. She could already hear Grey moving around in the kitchen – doing what, she had no idea. It was all she could do to lean back against the door. Everything was suddenly such an effort now the first rush of fear had worn off.

All the way back to the Barbican, she'd felt as though her heart was in her mouth and that was the only thing that had kept her from screaming. The idea that if she opened her lips wide enough to scream, her heart would tumble out and on to the pavement. But it had done whatever it was supposed to do, and it had propelled her back up Carthusian Street and inside the solid concrete walls. She still felt numb.

Was it shock, or was it just another side effect of the pills? Noah had said they did something to adrenaline, hadn't he?

Noah.

What had happened to him? Was he dead, too? Was he just lost or missing and scared? Was he hiding? Was he hurt?

And Mia – what about her? Izzy had already tried her phone. It went straight to voicemail.

The only good thing was that it wasn't Mia's mobile they heard ringing in the building site, but then, if it was there, how would they know? What if two of their friends were lying hidden behind the boards, and Izzy and Grey had been standing within reach? What if Noah was bleeding into the ground even as Grey laid his hands on the hoarding – separated by only a thin piece of board that might as well have been an ocean.

No. It was too much.

She squeezed her eyes shut and tried to pretend she didn't still see what was left of Juliet. And when she opened her eyes and there, out of the window, she saw Juliet's corpse dangling from the balcony above, she could only manage a small sound in the back of her throat. The body spun slowly in the breeze. It rotated enough to reveal the end of the metal hook jutting out through the back of her neck, smeared with red and splinters of shockingly white bone. As Izzy stared at it, the corpse raised its head and twisted its broken neck to look around at her. It blinked through its glasses.

Izzy fought another urge to throw up.

The world flickered again and adjusted itself – and the body disappeared.

Not that that made her feel much better. In fact, it made her feel like she was losing her mind.

"What are you looking at?" Grey was standing in the hallway from the kitchen, watching her.

"You don't want to know."

She followed him through into the kitchen, where she rummaged out clean mugs, remembering the promise she'd made to herself that she was done with coffee. Maybe she'd have to take a break from that, at least for the next thirty-six hours or so. The way she saw it, coffee was all that stood between her and, well, Bad Things.

"So what now?" She flicked the switch on the coffee machine and turned to find Grey leaning his head against one of the kitchen cupboards. He looked over at her blearily, not even lifting his forehead from the cupboard door.

"Dunno." He looked back down again.

"It was your idea to come here…"

"You have a better one?"

"No."

"Right, then." He blinked slowly at his feet – one, two, three times. All the energy seemed to have drained from him.

"Are you feeling OK?"

"Nope. Not OK. Not even close." He rolled away from the cupboard, then leaned back against it, rubbing his eyes with both hands. "My head hurts. It hurts so much. It's like there's a little guy in there sticking me with a spike." He took the mug of coffee she handed him. "I was doing all right, you know? I was holding it together. Even with all this –" he waved a hand vaguely – "crap."

Crap didn't quite cover it, somehow.

He downed the hot coffee and winced. "And then there was the thing with Juliet, and now Noah and …

222

I don't even know any more." His eyes met hers and all Izzy could see was despair. "Maybe we should just give up now. We're screwed either way, aren't we?"

"That's not what Noah thought…" Izzy took a sip of her own coffee and immediately regretted it – it was far too hot. How had Grey drunk his so easily?

"Noah's dead."

"We don't know that."

"Yeah, we do." He pointed to the window on the far side of the kitchen – the one looking towards Smithfield. Sure enough, there were blue lights flashing everywhere. Izzy slid open the balcony door and stepped outside, peering down at the street. Two police cars had pulled up across each of the roads leading towards the market, blocking them off – the roads they had all covered earlier. A cluster of emergency vehicles were parked at the nearest corner of the market building; the blue lights strobed off the little tower that marked the edge of the roof. Another cluster crowded around the next corner, too. The one at the bottom of Carthusian Street, right beside the building site.

"Oh," she said. Her fingers gripped the balcony rail more tightly.

"They're not there just for laughs, are they?" said Grey from inside. He had picked up the remote for the television and was jabbing buttons. As Izzy slipped back inside and closed the balcony door, the screen flared into life showing the road outside, and a woman's voice filled the room.

"…from Smithfield, right in the heart of London, where police have discovered the bodies of two local school students…"

Grey hit the mute button and the voice evaporated. "Question is, which two?" he muttered darkly.

The live footage disappeared and was replaced by a split-screen of two photographs.

Juliet and Noah.

Izzy recognized the pictures immediately. Both of them were in their Clerkenwell uniforms – they were the pictures from the last school portrait day.

"Oh, no." Her hand flew to her mouth. "School."

"School," Grey echoed. "And that's not the worst part."

The photos cut away to another live shot. The reporter was hurrying past the police cordon and down towards the building site, glancing over her shoulder to the camera as she went. The picture bounced and rolled as the cameraman tried to keep up, then steadied as a trolley with a body bag on top of it was wheeled away and into a waiting van, its windows blacked out and 'Private Ambulance' printed in sombre lettering on the side.

"Noah." Izzy's voice was barely even a croak as the live feed cut to something else. This time, it was footage – obviously recorded minutes before – of the inside of the building site. The hoardings had been peeled open, and whoever was holding the camera was standing at the top of the newly dug borehole for the tunnel, looking down. A man wearing orange high-vis clothing and a hard hat was being lowered on ropes into the hole. The edges of metal reinforcing mesh poked out of the soil around him, snagging at the ropes. And below him was a large blue tarpaulin, hastily unfolded and surrounded by a ring of vertical steel reinforcing bars. It was smeared with mud, and with blood, and although the hole was dark and the way the tarp draped was meant to hide the truth, anyone could see there was a body underneath it.

The camera shifted slightly as the rescue worker reached the bottom of the hole and moved the edge of the tarpaulin, peeling it back to reveal the top of a head of sandy brown hair, matted with blood. Noah.

It hit Izzy what must have happened. The ring of steel. The way the tarpaulin lay. Noah had been impaled on one of the steel reinforcing bars.

"You know what they're going to say, don't you?" Grey stared at the television screen.

"They're going to say that…" Izzy couldn't bring herself to say it.

"They're going to say that Noah did that to Jools. They're going to say he did it. That he killed her, and then he … he…"

"They can't!" Izzy's mouth dropped open in horror. "It's not true!"

He gave her an odd look. "You sure about that? It sure as hell plays that way, doesn't it?"

"You don't really think that."

"What do I think? I think that you're seeing things that aren't there, and you're doing things you don't remember. I think that Dom turned up dead and we don't know how. I think that the last time we heard from Noah, he was losing his mind. I think that he had the most to lose if Juliet told her parents. So, you know what? I don't have a damn clue what I should be thinking right now, but if I was a reporter, a scholarship kid under pressure at school killing one of his classmates, maybe two, right *here*? It's one hell of a story."

Izzy slumped into the closest chair. It was her favourite — a huge, soft thing covered in patchwork velvet and heaped with cushions. She always felt safe there, always felt happy. Or she always had, up till now.

Now, it was just another thing that used to be good and never would be again.

"We can't fix it, can we?"

"We can't fix it." Grey turned off the television as it cut back to the news reporter on the street again. Neither of them needed to see any more. He tossed the remote on to the sofa, then perched on the edge and rested his head in his hands. "We have to choose," he said from behind his fingers.

"Choose what?" Izzy hugged a cushion tightly to her chest.

"Between the others and ourselves." He dropped his hands and looked right at her. "Somebody's working their way through the group, and I don't care what Noah thought about the way Dom died. Juliet didn't do that to herself. And Noah?

227

He didn't… He didn't…" He bit his lip and stopped. There were tears welling up in his eyes – tears he obviously didn't want her to see, because he blinked hard and cleared his throat. "We're in trouble, Iz."

"Tell me something I don't know."

"We can hole up here, lock the doors, stay awake. That at least keeps us safe from whoever's out there. If Noah was right about the forty-eight-hour thing, we'll be fine…"

"*Fine.* You mean fine, apart from all our friends being dead."

He didn't answer.

"What's the alternative?"

He didn't answer for a long, long time. When he did, he sounded as tired as he looked. "We find the others. Whatever happens, we find the others."

Izzy turned the idea over in her head. Mia could be anywhere – if she was still alive. They could waste hours looking for her and putting themselves right in the path of whoever had stuck a hook through Juliet's throat. She shivered, and right on cue, Juliet was there again. This time, she wasn't hanging from the balcony above. This time, she was standing on the balcony and looking in. Her neck was twisted, the skin around it loose. As Izzy watched, she slowly raised one of her hands and pressed it against the glass.

"I'm losing my mind." It was a relief to say it out loud. Grey barely even flinched.

"You and me both."

"I can see Juliet."

"What's she doing?"

"I think she wants to come inside."

"When we found her..." He stumbled over the words. "When the lights came on? I didn't realize it was her. She didn't look like her. Not at first."

"Who was it?"

"It was *you*, Iz. I saw you hanging up there."

"Me?"

Juliet's mangled hand tapped lightly on the window, and Izzy turned away.

"Juliet's parents, they work in the hospital. So does Noah's mum, right? She's a nurse. Every day, they're going to see Noah's mum and they're going to think—"

"Stop it, Iz," Grey snapped. "There's no point."

"But we know what's really happening. We have to say something. We *have* to!"

"Why? So we can watch our lives go up in smoke, too? What about *our* parents? What do you think they're going to say when we tell them we took those pills; that we're involved in all this?"

She was about to tell him that she knew how that kind of conversation went, and she never wanted to go through it again. But she stopped herself. Luckily, he didn't seem to notice her hesitation. "No!" she said angrily, hoping it covered what she'd been thinking.

"Right, then." He softened a little. "Let's just get through the next few hours, all right? Once we're sure we're not going to go completely gaga – permanently – we'll figure out what to do. Besides –" he smiled sadly – "if we walk into a police station and tell them that you're seeing evil nurses and dead people, and I'm seeing people who are standing right next to me swinging from steel cables, we're going to end up in a nice comfy padded room. And probably shot full of tranquillizers. And you know what that means."

Izzy knew very well what it meant. It meant a cell just like the one in the video. And an ending just like it, too.

Maybe that's how he'd got there in the first place. Maybe he'd asked for help...

Grey was right. They had to get through this first. Then they could maybe start figuring out a way to clear up the mess they'd found themselves in.

If they got through this.

"We should still try and call them," she said.

Grey shook his head. "They haven't called us. Well. They haven't called *you*. All they'll get if they try me is a fish."

Of course, his phone was somewhere in the lake, wasn't it? "Tigs is much more likely to try calling you than me."

"Yeah, well. She never gives up." There was something that looked suspiciously like a smirk on his face.

"Should she?"

"Why d'you want to know?" Grey grinned and winked at her. It was, for a second, beautifully normal and she could almost believe it was the same as any other time they'd crashed out on her sofa to watch horror films all night. Almost the same, anyway. Only this time, *they* were the ones in the horror film, weren't they?

Grey pushed his hands back through his hair. "Executive decision, I'm going to the bathroom."

"Thanks. Probably more information than I needed."

"That wasn't what I actually meant to say – although I am going to the bathroom. What I meant was – executive decision. We hole up here for now, at least. I don't love the idea of running round in the dark, and you know what this place is like at night."

She did. The Barbican, once any events had finished and the Centre itself had closed for the night, was creepy at the best of times. Now, from the safety of the apartment, even the thought of venturing back out on to deserted, shadow-filled walkways outside was terrifying.

"So. I reckon we're going to need more coffee. Stick the machine on, yeah?"

"You know where the kitchen is." She tried not to sound offended.

Grey shrugged. "I'm going in the other direction, though, aren't I?" And with that, he sauntered off down the hallway to the bathroom at the far end.

"Unbelievable…" Izzy muttered, shaking her

head and very deliberately not looking at the windows. She rinsed out mugs and pressed the buttons on the coffee machine with shaking fingers, and generally bashed about in the kitchen the same way she always did when Grey was there. She heard the bathroom door unlock and heard him coming back down the hallway towards the kitchen. The coffee maker gurgled and she turned to check it and seeing movement out of the corner of her eye, she glanced over at the doorway to the hall. Grey was standing there in the half-light, silent. Watching her. His eyes followed everything she did and he looked so serious again that it worried her.

"What's up?" she asked, pouring milk into the coffee. He didn't answer. "Did something happen?"

Grey simply leaned against the doorframe and smiled at her.

It wasn't a nice smile.

"Grey? You're scaring me…" Izzy put the milk down and dropped her hand, feeling for the handle of the closest kitchen drawer. The drawer where the knives were kept. She could feel herself starting to tremble. "Seriously, you're beginning to freak me out."

He still didn't reply. Only kept on watching her, smiling at her.

"Grey!"

From somewhere at the other end of the apartment, there was the sound of a lock clicking and a door opening; of footsteps coming back down the hallway. Grey's voice drifted in from the living room.

"How're we looking with that coffee, then?"

Izzy's hand froze halfway to the drawer.

Grey was in the living room.

But he was also in the kitchen doorway.

"Iz? Did you call me?" A second Grey, the Living-Room-Grey, appeared from the hallway – and the two of them were suddenly side by side in the doorway. The one who had been there all along, the fake Grey, cocked his head on one side and sneered at the real version of himself. He raised his hand to his neck and slowly drew a finger across his throat.

"Iz, look at me," the real Grey said quietly.

"I am." Her hands were shaking so violently that she had altogether given up on being able to open the drawer – and what was she going to do with a knife, anyway?

She jerked away from the drawer, from the knives,

from everything so abruptly that she knocked over one of the mugs. It shattered, sending shards of china scattering across the worktop and spilling boiling hot coffee over the edges and on to the floor. The last drips caught the light as they fell, and Izzy could see the toe of a leopard-print shoe peeking around the edge of the doorway…

"Hey." Grey was beside her, holding a washing-up cloth. "You're safe. It's fine."

"I'm not, and you're not — and nothing's fine. Nothing's fine. It just isn't."

"I've got this. Drink the coffee." He pointed to the remaining mug. "You're going to need it."

"I'll make another one."

"No. You'll drink that because you look like crap, and I need you to stay awake. I can make my own coffee. Besides, yours is terrible." He dropped the cloth on the floor and started to mop up the worst of the puddle by poking it around with his foot while he handed her the full mug, closing her hands around it just to make sure. "It's going to be a long night, and an even longer day tomorrow."

As she walked stiffly back into the living room, still shaking enough that she had to concentrate on not spilling her coffee, from the corner of her eye she saw the fake Grey walking along the hallway, his hands in his pockets. He stopped outside her bedroom door, turned and gave her a cold smile. And then he vanished.

Chapter Fifteen

Izzy had wanted to put the news on again to see if there was anything more about Noah and Juliet – or about the others. Grey snatched the remote from her hand. "Trust me," he said, "we'll know. One way or another."

So they watched films, just like they had so many times before. Like everything was normal. Old black and white movies, Izzy's slasher films (although even Grey admitted those suddenly felt a little too real for comfort) and ghost stories. They watched vampire films and films with monsters; films with terrible lines and worse effects, in which people screamed and cried and ran for their lives, but none of them looked like they felt the same way Izzy did. None of them seemed numb. None of them seemed to be lost. They were scared, sure, but at least they knew what to do. They ran out of the house, or away from the abandoned mine. They hit the killer in the head with a shovel or blew up the mad scientist's lab. There was always something they could do.

What could she do? Where could she run to, to hide from the things that were in her own head? And, worse, what else would she see? What else *could* she see?

Izzy knew perfectly well that neither of them were actually watching the films. They were a way of passing time, of staying awake. Nothing more. They had argued for hours. About whether they should go to the police, whether they should go to the hospital. Whether there was anything they could have done. Whether they could have saved Juliet or Noah. Whether there had been someone coming for them, too. Whether there still was. Whether they should be afraid. Because she was. She was afraid.

She leaned back into the cushions of the sofa. However soft they were, there was no getting away from the fact that she was bone-achingly tired. Her ribs felt tender and her skin prickled under her clothes, like it was too small for her. When she stretched, her spine popped and clicked, and then felt stiffer than ever. Her eyes were so scratchy they might as well have been full of sand. Blinking, seeing, trying to focus on anything – they all hurt. When she looked away from the television screen at Grey, she could feel every muscle behind her eyes trying to refocus on him – a series of short, painful spasms and tugs inside her face. The cut on her cheek was still stinging from the antiseptic she'd cleaned it with, too. Her whole face felt like there were bugs crawling under her skin.

Grey didn't seem to be faring any better. He slumped on the sofa and stared blankly at the screen. Every now and again, he blinked slowly. The rims of his eyes were even redder than before, and he was so pale. His skin looked paper-thin – thin enough to see the veins beneath it if she looked closely enough and to make out the thin white scar across the bridge of his nose. She'd always meant to ask him how he got it. Maybe she should have – it didn't look like she was going to get the chance now.

"Would you do it again?" she'd asked as the figures on the television screen ran and screamed and hid and stabbed.

"Do what again?"

"Take the pills."

"Are you crazy? Of course not!"

"I mean, if it didn't go like this. If they were just … pills. And if they worked and nobody would know and nobody died."

"That's a lot of ifs."

"I'm just trying to make conversation."

He fidgeted in his seat. "I don't know. I guess I'm supposed to say no. Because it's cheating."

"But you're not going to, are you?"

"I don't know. All I know is that I feel like I'm in one of these –" he nodded to the screen – "and I put myself right there. You know the bit where the girl's walking up the stairs in the empty house, even though she thinks that's where the serial killer's hiding? And you're shouting at her not to do it? I feel like I'm watching myself walk up the stairs. It's going to end badly and it's all my own fault."

"So … that *is* a no."

"Huh." He looked thoughtful. "Maybe it is."

"Yeah. Me, too."

She risked a glance at the window. There was nobody there, dead or otherwise, and the flicker of blue light thrown up from the police cars and ambulances on the street had long since stopped. They were all still there, of course, but the Barbican tended to be home to the kind of people you didn't want to risk keeping awake all night with flashing lights.

Above the market, the sky had moved through shades of black and dawn-pink and orange and finally into the bright blue of tomorrow. Already it was beginning to bleach into the hot white of a London summer's day.

"Do you blame Tigs?" Izzy couldn't stop herself from asking the question. It just sort of fell out of her, and she was surprised by how scratchy her voice sounded.

"What for?"

"The pills. This."

"I want to." Grey paused. "I really do want to. But it's not her fault, is it? She was just being Tigs. With her, there's always an easy fix. Always has been. In her world you chuck money at something until it goes away, and if it doesn't you chuck pills at it so it doesn't bother you any more. Sometimes you do both. That's not her fault, either. She just doesn't know any other way. As far as she's concerned, everyone can be bought with something."

"Is that why she has so much trouble with you?"

"Yeah. She just hasn't found my price yet." He did his best to grin.

Izzy thought for a moment. "There'll be police about, won't there?"

"I guess."

"So at least we shouldn't have to worry about somebody coming after us."

"That's what scares you the most, is it?" He slid forward to the edge of the sofa and rested his elbows on his knees, rubbing at his face like he was drying it with an invisible towel.

"No…" The truth was, she didn't know. At first, it had been the video that scared her – the thought that the FokusPro could turn any of them into *that*. Then she had seen Juliet, seen Dom… And now she didn't know what should scare her the most. "No," she said again.

"Right, then." He stood up and stretched, yawning. Izzy fought back the urge to yawn, too. "We must be down to less than twenty-four hours by now?"

"Something like that."

"See? Piece of cake. All we have to do is not go crazy and not die." He was doing his best to grin at her, but it came out more as a lopsided sort of scowl.

He yawned again. "I think half my face has gone to sleep."

"As long as it's just your face," she said pointedly, collecting a bunch of empty coffee mugs from the table. "Can you overdose on coffee?"

"Dunno. But at about 1am, I thought my heart was about to explode."

"Maybe that's a better way to go."

"Wow. You're just a bundle of joy, aren't you?"

"Sorry." She shrugged and stumbled through into the kitchen. Her phone was sitting on the worktop. "Should we try calling them now?"

"I was just thinking the same." He followed her, and leaned against the doorway in an unsettling echo of the night before.

"Then I thought that it's too early, and they'd all be asleep, but…"

"*But*. Exactly. Time doesn't make a whole lot of sense any more, does it?" He scooped up her phone and tossed it to her. She almost dropped the phone twice, as she tried to catch it.

"Who? Mia or Tigs?"

"Better make it Tigs. She'll sulk if we call Mia first, and I can't face the thought of her being sulky *and* sleep-deprived." Grey was apparently refusing to take the situation seriously. Izzy couldn't decide whether that made her love him or hate him.

Tigs didn't answer her phone. "Maybe the battery's flat," Izzy said, as she hung up from Tigs's voicemail.

"Maybe she's dead."

"Grey!"

"Look, it's something we're going to have to think about. I mean, we chose to stay here and not go looking for them. You have to face facts. We might be the only two left."

Without warning, the room wheeled around her. Everything was spinning and there was a high-pitched sound in her ears. Grey's words may as well have been a slap. What if they *were* the only two left? What if, by locking themselves away with coffee and, of all things, old horror movies, they had left the others to their fate? She no longer felt numb – she felt sick. Sick and dirty and guilty.

The ringing noise faded out in time for her to hear the end of Grey's little spiel. "…our story straight."

"What?"

"I said, we need to figure out what we're going to

say. To tell people. You know, if it ends up with just us."

"No."

"No?"

"No."

"What part of this don't you get, Iz?"

"The part where we just ditch our friends and leave them to die – and then lie about it. No."

"Have you got a better idea?"

"Yes." She backed away from the worktop. The floor beneath her felt soft, spongey. If she trod on it too heavily, if she wasn't careful, it would swallow her. "We go and find them."

"Izzy…"

"You can stay here if you want. I can't. I shouldn't have in the first place." She spun to face him, only just keeping her balance. "We should have all stuck together."

"You're going. That's it?"

"That's it. Let's hope we're not too late." She didn't wait for him to answer or to see whether he would follow, but pushed past him and out through the front door.

245

In the lobby, the porter was having an argument with a couple of lift mechanics.

"No, I'm sorry, but you're not leaving them like that. We can't be two lifts down for that long." He nodded to her as she hurried past, then went back to arguing about shutting down the lifts. It sounded like the argument had been going on for some time. As she shouldered open the heavy glass door and stepped out into the day, the summer air wrapped around her. It still smelled clean, fresher than it would by the end of the afternoon when the traffic fumes had built up, and the cars and buses kicked up all the day's dust from the roads. The usual sounds of the lorries leaving Smithfield, of the market packing up and closing down, were missing – everything had been shut down the second they discovered Juliet.

Juliet. Izzy found herself looking around, just in case, but she was still alone. Behind her, the door to the lobby of Lauderdale banged, and by the sound of the footsteps hurrying after her, it had to be Grey. Obviously he'd decided that she was right. Either that or he didn't want to be left by himself. The memory of the second Grey, the fake Grey, flickered through her mind, but that Grey had made a lot less noise than the real one.

From Lauderdale's forecourt, Izzy could see the roof of Juliet's house. If she stood on tiptoe and looked all the way across the gardens and the lake, she would be able to see the waterfall where, with a shudder, she realized Dom must still be lying. She could see the balcony of Mia and Dom's apartment, where Noah had told them everything. It felt like it was days ago; weeks. And the party in the garden had been a different life – someone else's. It had been a dream, and this? This was a nightmare.

Grey was now looking down at Juliet's house, too. His hands in the pockets of his jeans and his shoulders slouching forward.

"Let's try Tigs," she said, and Grey nodded silently.

They took the steps up to the main level of the Barbican – the podium, which acted as a sort of raised ground floor. They reached the top of the steps together, standing aside to let a knot of tourists hurry past on their way to Barbican Tube station. A woman with long blonde hair appeared from behind a column, almost crashing into them. She squeaked with surprise. "Sorry! I'm just trying to work out the way to the Tube?" Her fringe fell into her eyes as she looked from one to the other of them, and Izzy wondered what she saw. Grey smiled and pointed to the thick yellow line painted on the ground.

"Just follow that," he said. The woman nodded her thanks and hurried off.

The yellow line was, like many things in the Barbican, a running joke to residents – it snaked around the more public walkways and was supposed to guide visitors through the labyrinth, either to the Barbican Centre or to the exits on to the street, but all it usually did was confuse everyone even more. In some places it had been worn away; in others, it disappeared into a solid wall. Once, in a far corner of the Barbican, someone had got hold of a can of paint in exactly the same shade of yellow and had cheerfully drawn impossible-to-follow lines that went up walls, over balconies and across the ceilings of some of the walkways. For a while, it had been funny to hang around nearby and watch the baffled tourists try to figure out how to climb vertical concrete. This time, however, the yellow line seemed to be doing its job and the lost woman headed off towards the station.

"What do we do if Tigs isn't home?" Grey asked the question Izzy had been trying not to think about.

"I guess we try Mia's. Or Kara's."

"Kara's place is right by that building site, Iz. I don't think we're getting anywhere near it."

"Well, then." Izzy stopped walking. "Did you hear that?"

"Hear what?"

"That sound." She cocked her head sideways, straining to pick it up again. There had definitely been something – it had sounded like someone calling her name.

"Nope."

"Weird."

"Ignore it. You know it's just in your…" Grey tailed off. He was staring ahead of them, at the covered walkway that ended beside Shakespeare Tower. The exact spot where Izzy had walked into him while trying to get away from her invisible stalker. "You don't…" He stopped and started again. "You don't see someone standing there, do you? Watching us?"

Izzy stared into the mouth of the tunnel so hard that she started to see spots. Shadows moved and green splodges swirled across her vision, but there certainly wasn't a person there. Grey, however, kept looking.

"There was a guy there, all dressed in black. He was looking at us, I swear. And then he moved back against the wall and I lost him."

"You're sure he's real?"

"Tell me, Iz. When you've seen things – and I mean *seen* them – have they looked like just some random dude leaning against a wall?"

"Not exactly…" Only, she thought, if the random dude was peeling off his own face.

"Come on," said Grey, and without warning he took her hand, tugging her forward.

"What…?" Izzy didn't get the chance to object any further as he was dragging her towards the walkway. It gaped at them, ready to swallow them both. Had it always been so dark? She couldn't remember. Everything was harder to remember. The soles of her feet ached with each step they took and yet Grey pulled her along with him, determined.

"I'm telling you – I saw someone."

"Did you? Did you *really*, or do you just think you did?"

He didn't reply.

Perhaps it was because she didn't usually walk through the tunnel from this end, she'd always just used it as a shortcut home from the Barbican Centre, but now, it felt wrong. It felt odd and off-kilter. The ventilation slats that covered the walls looked closer together than usual and sharper, too. The pools of light filtering down from the lightwells looked sickly and everything seemed to be pressing in on them. Was the ceiling always so low?

"I don't like this."

"Shh." He was still peering straight ahead – she was just a passenger as far as he was concerned. Maybe he had seen someone. Maybe there was someone watching them. Maybe there had been all along, and maybe whoever it was wanted them dead… But how could you tell what was real and what wasn't? The scalpel cut on Izzy's cheek began to sting again as she struggled to keep pace with Grey. Her fingers hurt where he held them, he was holding on to her so tightly. Too tightly.

With frightening speed, Grey dropped her hand, then whipped around and grabbed her by the shoulder, nearly lifting her off her feet as he slammed her back against the vents. Hot air rushed down her back, blowing her hair out around her face and into her eyes.

"What are you doing?" she shouted over the hum of the fans.

He didn't answer — didn't even show any sign that he'd heard her — and just kept her pressed against the sharp metal edges of the louvres with his fist. His eyes were flat and cold. The warmth had gone from them and all that was left was steel-grey. Whatever he was seeing, it wasn't her.

"Grey!"

There wasn't even a flicker of recognition on his face. Nothing. He was a stranger. It was his face, yes, but the person looking back at her was somebody else. And he was not her friend.

"Let me go…" She pulled forward, trying to wriggle out of his grip, but with a sudden jerk of his hand he shoved her back again. Her head caught the edge of one of the vents and the world became suddenly fuzzy, blackening around the edges. She was going to faint. She couldn't faint. Fainting counted as going to sleep, didn't it? If she fainted…

The darkness clogged her vision, and still he held her. The fingers of his free hand were clenching, unclenching. Clenching, unclenching.

Everything was going dark. Her knees couldn't hold her up much longer – if he let go, she would fall.

His free hand.

She had a free hand, too.

Blinking back the dark, she raised her hand – and she slapped him across his cheek.

Startled, he stepped back, releasing her, and she slumped to the floor.

Still seeing stars from the knock to her head, she shook herself, trying to clear her vision. Grey just stood there and blinked down at her. Would he recognize her now? Was he himself again?

She wasn't going to stick around to find out.

Scrabbling for grip on the floor of the walkway, she dragged herself to her feet and turned and ran for all she was worth.

Izzy ran, even though her body ached and her head was pounding. Even though her heart was beating so fast she thought it would split open. The sound of her feet echoed all around her, and she couldn't tell whether his footsteps were there, too. She skidded to a halt in front of a side door to the Centre and pushed through it, still running. People stared at her as she passed, but she didn't care. She ran to the stairs and piled down them until she ran out of steps on the lakeside level. Tumbling out of the stairwell, she looked around desperately for somewhere she could go, somewhere she could hide until whatever it was that had got into Grey passed. If it did pass.

An idea hit her, and she was running again — this time for the wide, shallow stairs in the middle of the Centre, down to the theatre and the cloakrooms. It was the only place she could think of. She raced down the stairs to the lowest level of the Barbican and looked around. It was deserted. Suddenly, being alone didn't seem like the best idea.

The frosted glass door to the women's toilets was right in front of her, and she ran for it. Somewhere above her, she thought she heard someone calling her name again.

The door swung closed behind her with a gentle *swoosh*. She was alone. She was safe. For now.

Groaning, she leaned on the nearest sink and let the water run; splashing water on to her face. It wasn't him, she knew that. It wasn't Grey's fault, exactly…

He really hadn't known it was her.

He could have done *anything*.

Yet again, the image of Juliet flashed in front of her, swinging from the hook and cable, and the conversation she'd had with Grey echoed in her ears.

They're going to say that Noah did that to Jools.

They can't! It's not true!

For the first time, Izzy began to wonder whether he'd been right.

She could feel the sweat drying across her face, feel her skin tightening underneath it. Her hands wouldn't stop shaking, no matter how hard she tried to steady them. The water spluttered and then began to flow smoothly again, pouring into the basin as a cool and steady stream. She splashed more of it on to her face, rubbing wet fingers across the back of her neck and across her forehead. Anything to make herself feel better. Breathing deeply, she closed her eyes and leaned her head on the mirror over the sink.

"It's fine. You're fine. All fine," she whispered to herself.

It was working. Her lungs were no longer screaming for air and her heart didn't feel like someone was flamenco dancing up and down the inside of her ribcage. She pushed the thoughts of Juliet and Noah out of her head. She had to, however bad she felt about doing it. This was about her now.

"OK. All fine," she said, pulling away from the mirror and opening her eyes.

The porcelain of the sink was streaked with black. She held up a hand in front of her face – that, too, was covered in something black and sticky like tar. The water pouring from the tap wasn't water any longer, and it didn't pour – it oozed thickly, splattering the sides of the sink with a noxious-smelling liquid. Slowly, Izzy raised her eyes to the mirror…

Her face was covered in it; it was smeared through her hair and round her throat. Her hands dripped with it. The smell, something part chemical, part animal, made her gag. She tried to turn it off, her fingers slipping on the metal, but the tap wouldn't budge. If anything, it came faster and faster until it was not just splattering the sink but filling it with sludge. The stench was overwhelming and it was *everywhere*. Desperately, Izzy fumbled with the tap, pulling on it again and again until it began to turn. Slowly at first, then more and more, until the flow of sludge slowed to a drip and then stopped altogether.

Her heart pounding just as heavily as it ever had, Izzy looked up at her reflection in the mirror again.

It was clean.

So was the sink.

There was nothing there but splashes of water, and a lingering smell that could have been the drains.

Pulling a handful of paper towels from the dispenser, she dried her hands and face, and took yet another deep breath to calm herself. That hadn't been fun. None of it was fun. Besides, she couldn't stay in the bathroom all day, could she? The longer she stayed there, the less safe she was. And what about Grey? She felt a twinge of guilt. Hadn't she just told him that they needed to find the others and stay together? And then hadn't she just run away and left him? What was she *thinking*?

"You were thinking that you didn't want to get yourself killed, let alone have Grey be the one that did it. Seems fair enough to me. How's your mind holding up, by the way? Still feeling sane?"

She froze.

The voice that had spoken – had answered the question she hadn't actually said out loud – was hers.

But Izzy hadn't even opened her mouth.

Chapter Sixteen

Izzy turned slowly towards the voice. It had come from the far end of the row of cubicles.

Her voice. *Hers*.

She looked.

One side of the bathroom was taken up by the row of toilet cubicles, the other by a line of sinks and mirrors with one larger, floor-to-ceiling mirror taking up the whole of the far wall. Izzy could see herself reflected in it, staring back out. But there was no door reflected behind her – and then her reflection took a step forward.

It wasn't a mirror at all, it was an archway through into the next section of the bathroom.

And she wasn't seeing a reflection. She was seeing … something else.

She spun on her heel, desperate to get to the door, but a hand reached over Izzy's shoulder from behind and slammed it shut again.

"Nuh-uh," said the voice in her ear, and she turned to face herself.

The Izzy she was looking at was grinning unpleasantly at her. There was a vivid white mark on her cheek where real Izzy knew the scalpel cut was on her own face, and her lips were tinged with blue. The fingernails of the hand that was holding the door shut were longer, broken, dirty, and her hair was lank and matted. The drain smell in the bathroom was stronger, the usual air freshener mingling with something else – a smell of rotten meat and damp wood.

"Can't run from yourself, can you?"

"You're not real. I'm real."

"Is that what you tell yourself? What *is* real, anyway, when you get down to the guts and bones of it?"

"You. Aren't. Real."

"And how's that working out for you?" The imaginary Izzy wasn't listening, and Izzy recoiled as her double leaned closer and rubbed a cheek against her own. It was cold and unpleasantly clammy, and made Izzy think of a dead fish. The smell was almost overwhelming – even before the fake Izzy reached for her and ran a hand through *her* hair, trailing her fingertips across her face and lips. Izzy gagged, and before she could pull away, her double had forced her fingers into Izzy's mouth and clamped her other hand around the back of Izzy's head. A foul taste flooded her mouth as the other Izzy yanked her closer to her. Her grip was utterly pitiless as the tips of her fingers pressed further back into Izzy's mouth, stretching for her throat.

"Hey! Can you move away from the door please?" Someone was banging on the door – and with a rush of air into her lungs, Izzy found herself alone again. It – she, the hallucination, whatever it was – had vanished, and Izzy was left leaning heavily on the glass door with one hand. On the other side, the fuzzy outline of a woman wearing the Barbican Centre staff uniform shifted on the spot. Izzy dropped her hand and stepped back. The door swung open and the woman stepped briskly through it, carrying a roll of rubbish bags. She glared at Izzy.

"Sorry," Izzy panted. "Asthma."

"Mmm-hmm," said the woman, clearly not buying it. She elbowed Izzy out of the way and started rattling one of the rubbish bins around. Izzy took the opportunity to slip out of the bathroom and back into the Centre itself. The bottom level was still deserted, although now the sound of whistled show tunes drifted out of the ladies' toilets. There was still no sign of Grey, either waiting outside or on the stairs. She wasn't sure whether that was good or bad, but she knew she didn't want to trust him again just yet. Not until she was sure. Holding the handrail tightly, Izzy slowly pulled herself up the first flight of stairs. It was harder now. The wave of panic she'd felt in the bathroom had left her shaky and washed-out. Weak. She caught herself thinking that all she needed was a nap. Just an hour or so, and everything would be all right.

Everything looks better after a good night's sleep…

"Not going to happen," she told herself through gritted teeth.

Another cleaner on the floor above glanced up at her as she started on the second flight of stairs. He grinned. One of his front teeth was missing.

"Long night, love?" he called to her, cackling.

"You have no idea," she muttered. He carried on laughing as she made her way up to the ground floor of the Centre. After a quick glance around to check for ... well, anything, she went straight to the coffee stall in the middle and bought a bottle of water to wash the feeling of rot out of her mouth. It might all have been in her head but the taste of those long, cold fingers lingered just the same. As she swallowed the last of it, she caught sight of a familiar figure above her on one of the galleried walkways of the Centre's upper floors, looking down.

Grey.

Without thinking, she darted sideways behind a pillar. If he moved a little further along the walkway, he would be able to see her, but hopefully she would at least see him first. And in the meantime, she would just have to decide what she was going to do. As she stood there, trying to decide whether to call to him or hide, her phone beeped. Surprised, she rummaged it out of her pocket – she'd obviously found the one spot of reception in the Centre – at least, it was strong enough for a couple of messages to get through. There was a voicemail waiting on her phone.

It was Tigs, and although Izzy could only make out a few words, she could hear the panic in Tigs's voice. "Please ... up ... phone ... bad ... what to do

… are you? Please? Please, Izzy … me back."

Izzy listened to the whole message again, but she still couldn't make it out. As she hung up, there was another beep – a text. It was Tigs again, with just one word.

Help.

Risking a quick peep round the pillar, she could make out the back of Grey's head. He was looking the other way now, down to the far side of the Centre's ground floor. If she was quick, and if he didn't turn round, she should be able to get to the doors and out on to the lakeside. From there, all she had to do was go up the long flight of steps outside the Centre, cross the podium and she would be back where they'd been earlier – before Grey had flipped out, right in front of Shakespeare Tower. She reread the message on her phone, and looked back up at Grey on the walkway.

She would have to risk it.

Seeing him lean over the safety railing and peer down into the Centre, she took her chance, darting out from behind the pillar and towards the door. She had just made it through, and it was swinging shut behind her, when she heard him shout, "Izzy! Wait!"

She didn't wait, but she also knew that he would be expecting her to take the stairs. And, being Grey, he would catch her before she got anywhere near Shakespeare. She wasn't prepared to take *that much* of a risk.

Instead of taking the steps, she peeled away to the left, towards the lakeside entrance to the garden, and then turned sharply right underneath the steps. A gloomy doorway in the wall directly below the staircase opened into one of the underground car parks. It wasn't one she knew well. She'd only been down there once, soon after she'd moved to the Barbican, and that time she'd got hopelessly lost and had to backtrack all the way to the door. She was sure, though, that there was a residents' door to the bottom level of Shakespeare somewhere on the far side. All she had to do was find it, and then she'd be in.

She sidestepped a puddle of something dark that could have been water or could have been oil, and picked her way between parked cars, piles of rubbish sorted and left by the cleaners for recycling, and a shopping trolley with a notice tied to it, written in neat cursive script – *Please don't remove me.*

Somewhere nearby, there was a machine-hum – a power transformer or one of the motors for the Defoe House lifts directly above. Very far off, there were traffic sounds coming from the Beech Street tunnel that cut through the Barbican at street level, below the podium. Someone laughed and a phone rang – most likely somebody on the stairs up from the lakeside. Fumbling for her keys, Izzy headed deeper.

It got darker further in. The distances between the overhead lights got longer and the bulbs not as bright. There were fewer cars, too, and the ones parked here had a distinct air of neglect. Some of them were buried beneath car covers. Others had a thick layer of dust on their bonnets and windscreens. One, something old and vintage-looking, had a front tyre that was so flat it had pooled around the base of the wheel. Even the mechanical whirring sound had stopped here. There was nothing but thick, dust-covered grey silence.

The closest bulb in the ceiling flickered ominously. "Oh, of course you would," Izzy sighed at it. "Because I'm in a creepy and deserted car park all alone and nobody knows I'm here. Of *course* you'd start bloody flickering."

The light stopped flickering.

Izzy peered at it. "That told you, didn't it?"

Something moved on the floor, just at the edge of her line of sight. She felt her pulse quicken, felt her throat tighten with the surge of panic.

It was a mouse, scurrying from one shadow to the next. Not even a rat – just a mouse.

That was all it took. Izzy was so tired, so tense, so *everything*, that a small grey mouse could set her well on the way to a heart attack. "Mouse won't hurt you, Iz," she told herself, half expecting it to stop, turn round and growl at her. But it didn't. Instead, it disappeared under a pile of cardboard where it continued to make little scuffling, scratching sounds.

As the mouse crept away, she found herself starting to giggle – completely unexpectedly, just the way she'd felt the urge to laugh when they had found Juliet. It wasn't a normal sort of laugh, there was nothing happy about it. It was the kind of laugh that comes when everything is spinning out of control, when the horror and fear and the flat-out exhaustion are just too much to bear and all there is to do is either laugh, or scream until your voice gives out. Izzy knew that if she gave in this time, if she started to laugh, she might not be able to stop. Ever. She took a couple of deep breaths, in and out, to feel like she was in control again.

The fact that she was suddenly holding what appeared to be a rusty metal bar in her right hand, which had most definitely not been there a minute ago, and which she most certainly didn't remember picking up... That was probably a bad sign.

The bar fell to the floor with a loud clang as she let it go. Her hands felt sticky with rust and they smelled of wet metal. No cuts. No grazes or anything unexpected – not on her. There had been nobody else... Had there?

Where had the bar come from?

She needed to get to Tigs. But what if...?

It would only take a minute or two. She needed to know.

She doubled back through the car park, retracing her steps. It wasn't hard – she could see her footprints in the dust and grit that had settled on the floor. There was only one set, and she would recognize the patterns left by the soles of her canvas trainers anywhere. The footsteps went in a straight line from where she had ended up, as far back as the car with the flat tyre. And then they did something unexpected. They looped around the back of the car.

"That's not right…"

But it was right. Izzy's footprints went to the back of the car and then headed off across the car park in a completely different direction.

"That's definitely not right. I didn't come in that way." With a lump in her throat and something that felt like a fist wedged in her stomach, she tracked her path back across the car park. The dust wasn't as thick in this section, and the cars looked like they were actually used here, but it wasn't difficult to see where she'd been. All she had to do was follow the trail of broken glass.

The headlights of every car around her had been smashed. The glass littered the ground around her, glittering under the lights.

…broken glass that crunched under her feet…

"Oh, no."

The first thought that went through her head was, *How long have I been down here?* The second was a voice, almost forgotten.

You shouldn't be here, dearie…

It was that thought that really made her move.

Spinning around to get her bearings, she ran for the far side of the car park. There had to be a door up to Shakespeare somewhere. How long had she been down here? She wasn't sure. It wasn't like there'd been time to check her watch before she'd come in, she'd been in too much of a hurry. It could have been fifteen minutes; it could have been more or it could have been less. Either way, Tigs had needed her help.

She slid to a dead halt. The text from Tigs. It would be timestamped. Frantically, she dug out her phone. The screen glowed brightly in the dimly lit car park, the message still there in its little box. Izzy looked at the clock on the phone. She looked at the message in horror.

"An hour?"

That wasn't possible. It just wasn't. What had she been doing in a car park for an *hour*?

Besides the obvious...

The door to the lower level of Shakespeare Tower gave her the answer to that question when she finally found it. Like all the other doors to Barbican blocks, it was formed of a heavy, blue-painted metal frame around two panes of thick shatterproof glass. In this case, someone had done their best to smash the glass. Cobwebby cracks spread out across both panes where something hard had been swung at them with force. Something like, say, a metal bar. The same metal bar looked like it had been put to work on the lock as well – the barrel was smashed to pieces but the door stayed stubbornly locked.

There was no way Izzy was getting that door open. She'd already made sure of that.

"Why would I smash the lock?" she asked the empty car park. The palm of her right hand had started to throb, and rubbing it with her other thumb, she could feel blisters already forming beneath the skin. "I'm losing my mind. I'm *losing* my *mind*."

If there was no way up to Shakespeare, she could either turn right round and go back outside to the steps – perhaps even call Tigs from out there. Or she could try and find another door, up to Defoe House. It would at least take her up to the podium level, directly across from the bottom of Shakespeare, and that was better than nothing. As for Grey, by now he must have given up. Maybe he was back to normal. Maybe he'd gone to look for Tigs. Maybe he'd been able to help.

Or maybe…

"A lot can happen in an hour. What if you're the only one left?" she asked herself. "What then?"

There was one way to find out.

Chapter Seventeen

The lock to the Defoe House staircase worked just fine, and the door banged shut behind her as Izzy stepped into the stairwell. It was cold – surprisingly so, given how warm it was outside. But at least it was better lit than the car park. Apart from a small cork noticeboard beside the door out to the car park (covered in notes about piano lessons and not leaving recycling around the car park and encouraging mice, which was clearly being ignored by everyone) and the stairs themselves, there was nothing else to see. The sound of the door slamming echoed up and down the empty space.

As she set her foot on the first step, a wave of tiredness crashed over Izzy. Everything shimmered, sliding sideways and spinning away from her. She slipped, missing the step and falling. Her forehead caught the end of the metal handrail as she fell and connected hard. She hit the ground and curled into a tight ball, clutching her pounding head and trying not to lose her tenuous grip on her self-control.

"Get up, Izzy," she whispered. For once, she listened. Groaning, she shook her head to clear it and pulled herself back to her feet. The handrail, the metal banisters and the edges of the steps were all edged with fuzzy white stars that shifted as she blinked at them. The handrail suckered to her palms as she clung to it and tried to haul herself up the steps to the podium. Flakes of blue paint stuck to her skin.

Halfway up the stairs, she heard the hinges of the door behind her squeak, but there was no reassuring bang of the heavy door closing. There were no footsteps, no sounds of life or movement, but Izzy had just about stopped trusting what her senses told her. It didn't seem to mean a whole lot any more. She willed her sore limbs to move faster.

She had made it as far as the first landing when the shadow fell across the wall ahead of her. It was vaguely human-shaped, but even allowing for the angle of the lighting, there was no way anyone could have actually called it human. Its arms hung down to its knees and ended with grotesquely long, clawed fingers. Its head was slightly too large for its shoulders and it ducked its neck from side to side as it climbed the stairs behind her. She waited for it to do something – to lunge at her or to grab at her feet, but it simply stood there. It didn't try to come any closer or even to overtake her. It looked as though it was waiting for something. Izzy stopped climbing.

There was only one shadow – the twisted thing with the clawed hands.

So where was hers?

A stabbing pain behind her forehead made her flinch.

The monstrous shadow flinched.

Slowly, she raised a hand to rub at the spot that hurt.

The shadow raised its own horrible hand towards its face.

Not taking her eyes off it for one second, she stretched out her arms on either side of her. The shadow did the same thing, and gradually it shrank and shaped itself back around her.

Shaking, she lifted a hand and waved at the wall.

The shadow waved back.

The shadow was *hers*.

That smell. The smell like something rotting. The smell and that taste – the one that had lingered in her mouth after she'd seen herself in the bathroom. She'd come across it before, it was familiar.

It was the pills.

The same smell. The same taste.

And now there was no turning back.

With a burst of energy, she ran up the rest of the stairs and burst out of the door on to the podium level. A warm breeze caught her hair and blew it back from her face. Across from her was the entrance to Shakespeare Tower – she could see the door and the porter at his desk in the lobby. She realized she was standing in almost exactly the same spot she had been in with Grey earlier, right before he'd seen the figure lurking at the end of the walkway beside the bottom of Shakespeare. The same walkway she was looking at right now, and where someone was standing in the shadows. She took a step back. He took a step forward.

Grey.

Izzy couldn't tell whether he was back to normal again, but he was there. He was alive. Surely that could only be a good thing. He spotted her and was about to wave to her; he began to raise his arm when something made him look sharply up towards the top of the tower. Izzy, still beneath the overhang of the first floor of Defoe House, couldn't see what had caught his attention. She went to take a step forward again, but he waved back at her with both arms, and there was something desperate about it. He was warning her. Warning her about what?

The body hit the paving in front of her a heartbeat later.

It was the sound that bothered Izzy the most. Not the blood, nor the cracks that suddenly appeared in the pavement a few metres ahead of her. It wasn't the fragments of bone or even the pieces of what might have been a limb, only moments before, now blurred into a red mess. It was the sound it made as it landed – a wet, sucking, crunching noise, both solid and uncomfortably liquid, and surprisingly loud.

She was fairly sure her brain wouldn't have come up with a sound like that on its own, which meant this was more than just another hallucination.

This was real.

The porter jumped up from behind his desk and ran to the door. Izzy could see him frozen there, and she wondered whether he wasn't letting go of the door because he wanted to hold it open or because he wanted it to prop him up. Across the podium, she could see Grey's mouth opening and closing, but either no sound was coming out or she had lost the ability to hear it. Neither would have surprised her, because there was a body in front of her and it was spread over an area no human body should ever be.

Another stabbing pain behind her eyes made her double over, pressing her hand to her face. Even with her eyes closed, she could still see it. And when she opened her eyes again and dropped her hand, it was wet and red. There was blood all over her face. Blood all over her hand. Blood everywhere. Real blood. Not the kind she could pretend was just in her head. Not the kind that was just another sign she was tired and afraid and losing her mind. Real blood that belonged in a person. In a living, breathing human being.

Grey was running towards her. He had to get across the wet paving, slippery with what had been part of someone. His feet skidded and he almost fell more than once, but still he kept on coming. Izzy's feet felt like someone had nailed them to the ground. The idea of running now, of moving, of doing anything other than standing right where she was, was impossible. All she could do was stand. When he reached her, she saw just how bad Grey looked. His clothes were spattered with blood. His face, too. It stood out livid red against the greyish white of his skin. There were bruises across his nose and cheeks, and he had the beginnings of what looked like a solid black eye. She couldn't help herself – before he could say anything, before he could do anything, she reached out and touched it as gently as she could.

"The yellow line," he said softly.

"What?" Izzy blinked at him. Why was he bringing that up when there was something so much bigger, so much *worse*, to worry about? Who cared about the stupid yellow line?

"The yellow line. It tried to choke me. At least, I think it did. I don't know."

"The yellow line?" Izzy echoed, glancing down at the thick line of paint (now splashed with red) at their feet.

"Came alive."

"Ah." There wasn't much more to say.

"It's happening to me, isn't it? I did something. To you. I'm sorry…" Grey stumbled over the words.

"Not now."

"Izzy…"

"Not now." She could hear her voice – she sounded calm. Quiet. Strong. Detached – or numb. Distant. Empty.

Insane.

She nodded to the tower. "We can talk later. But not now."

"The porter, Iz. He saw it. If he saw it, it happened and he'll be calling the police."

"He's not at his desk right now, though, is he?" She pointed to the lobby of Shakespeare. It was deserted.

"Come on."

"You've got to be kidding me!" The look on Grey's face as he stared up at the building made it only too clear what he thought of that idea. "Izzy, someone either just fell off the top of Shakespeare Tower or was pushed. And you want to go up there?"

"Tigs left me a message. She was asking for help," Izzy said, her voice still remarkably, frighteningly calm.

Grey swore. Loudly. He kicked the pillar behind them. His foot left a dirty red scuff mark on the grey concrete. He dropped into a crouch and buried his head in his hands – and for a second Izzy almost thought she could hear sobbing. His back was heaving up and down with the effort of keeping control, of keeping his breathing steady.

"He's not going to be away from the desk forever," she said.

"I know." His voice was muffled by his hands. Slowly, he stood up and wiped his face. "You're right. We need to finish this."

The only way Izzy could bring herself to walk across the podium was by refusing to look down. If she didn't look down, she wouldn't see the wash of red, wouldn't see the shreds of body. Something crunched horribly beneath her foot and her stomach somersaulted inside itself, but she kept on walking. She didn't let herself start to wonder who it was that had fallen – if she did, she knew she'd never be able to get the memory of this, this walk, out of her head. She'd noticed how far away from it all she had begun to feel, like she was watching someone else do all these things. Everything was coming unravelled and yet again she caught herself wondering whether she wasn't just dreaming. Eventually, she decided that if this was all a dream (or a nightmare) then it was a pretty clear sign she needed some serious therapy. And if it was real, then she was definitely going to need that therapy once it was all over. Lots of it.

She'd never liked therapy.

The lobby, when they reached the door, was still empty. The porter was obviously still somewhere else – calling the police, calling an ambulance, throwing up. He didn't even appear when the lift pinged softly at them and the doors slid open. Grey staggered in, weaving slightly, but Izzy hesitated. The lift began to close, and Grey jabbed at the 'open door' button.

"It's OK," he said, holding his other hand out to her. "I'm not going to do anything."

"It's not you I'm worried about," she replied.

He blinked at her and almost dropped his hand – and for the first time, she saw the same uncertainty in his eyes that she already felt.

"Get in," he said finally.

She did.

They rode the lift up to Tigs's floor in silence, watching the numbers slide by.

Stick together, stay alive. Stick together, stay alive.

You shouldn't be here, dearie.

Take the pills. Take the pills. Take the pills the pills the pills…

There were voices in Izzy's head, rattling around and shouting over each other. All of them sounded like other people, and all of them sounded like her, and it was only because she could hear high-pitched laughter behind them all that she understood they weren't real.

She only had to hold it together for a few more hours.

A few more hours – and then what?

Well, there was sleep for a start.

Everything looks better after a good night's sleep…

The lift stopped. The doors opened and together they stepped out on to the landing. Izzy had no idea what she was expecting to find, but somehow the blank walls and closed doors were not it. It all looked so *normal*. Except the doors weren't all closed – the door to Tigs's apartment was open a crack. Out of the corner of her eye, she saw Grey's whole body tense. He raised a finger to his lips, warning her to be quiet. She rolled her eyes. Like she was planning on charging in there and making a racket...

They crept across the landing to the front door and flattened themselves against the wall beside it, listening. Everything seemed quiet. Grey reached out and pushed against the door with the flat of his hand, inching it open slightly and peering in. Murmured voices drifted out. They were too quiet for Izzy to understand what they were saying, but she was fairly sure they belonged to Mia and Kara. Tigs was never that quiet.

And if Mia and Kara were in Tigs's apartment...

In her mind's eye, Izzy saw Tigs sitting cross-legged on the podium paving, idly fingerpainting in the gore, her blonde hair streaked with red.

She shook the image away as Grey pushed the door open a little more and slipped inside. "What are you doing?" she hissed after him. He stuck his head back round the door.

"Kitchen," he whispered.

Something felt wrong and alarm bells were ringing

inside Izzy's head. Why were they sneaking in? Why was everything so quiet? If someone had just gone over the edge of the balcony, shouldn't there be more … *noise*?

The answer, she realized, was simple. Everyone was just too tired.

Everyone except Kara.

Kara hadn't taken the pills, so why was she there? And what was she doing?

The alarm bells rang a little louder, and she crept into the apartment behind Grey, carefully pulling the door back to its original position behind her.

The path to the kitchen was clear. Once they were sure they'd made it, they leaned against the walls on either side of the door, just as they had on the landing.

"What now?" she hissed as quietly as she could.

"We listen."

"What for?"

"I don't know. Anything. There's something off … I can—" He broke off abruptly and flattened himself even further against the wall as the voices got louder. They were somewhere at the far end of the apartment, in one of the bedrooms or the bathroom.

There was a crash, and the sound of something heavy slamming into something else – something like the walls or the floor. Shouting – Kara's voice, raised. A sharp sound like a slap.

Footsteps, running up the corridor towards them. Grey edged as far to the side as he could, gesturing for Izzy to do the same. She leaned away from the door, feeling the edge of the kitchen counter biting into her hip and willing herself smaller, barely daring to breathe.

A second set of footsteps, and the front door being pushed shut – hard. A lock turning.

Izzy's eyes met Grey's. They were locked in.

"I said, *give it to me!*" Mia was shouting, her voice boiling with rage. There was another crash, followed by a scuffle and something being smashed.

"No." It was Kara, but she sounded wrong. Her voice was thick and slow. She seemed to be having trouble speaking.

"Give it to me or I'll tear your tongue out right now!"

Izzy clamped her hands over her mouth as Mia spoke. Her voice was like ice, her words clear and suddenly cold. Across the doorway from her, Izzy saw how wide Grey's eyes were; how his hands had balled into fists.

In the hallway, Kara groaned. It sounded like she was trying to roll over or crawl away, and then she cried out sharply, suddenly.

Izzy couldn't take it any longer. She turned so that she was facing the wall, and slowly, carefully, quietly, edged around the side of the doorframe.

Kara was on the floor in the middle of the hallway, face down. Mia stood over her, her back to the kitchen. Her shoulders were hunched, and Izzy could see them heaving up and down. Her hands hung loosely by her sides and her fingers didn't stop twitching – even when she dropped her knees into the middle of Kara's spine, making her yell in pain. She reached for Kara's head, winding her fingers through her hair and tugging it sharply. And then she shifted, her back blocking Izzy's line of sight.

Mia leaned forward, pulling her elbow back to yank Kara's head up. "Tigs wasn't supposed to fall," she hissed. "She's no use to me dead."

"Then why did you—?" Kara's question was muffled, and cut off by Mia twisting another handful of her hair. She moaned in pain.

"She was supposed to go to *sleep*. *That* was the plan. I needed her." Mia sat back on Kara's spine, and shifted again.

Izzy could see Kara's head pulled back at a painful angle as Mia appeared to start braiding her hair.

"What the hell are you doing?" Grey hissed from the other side of the doorway.

"Shh." Izzy flapped a hand at him to be quiet as Mia froze and cocked her head to one side. Had she heard him?

Izzy held her breath and pulled her head back round the doorway.

Nothing happened.

After what felt like an hour, she risked another peek.

She'd been right – Mia was braiding Kara's hair. It even sounded like she was *humming* quietly to herself.

Mia, quite clearly, had completely lost her mind.

And now she was dangerous.

"When you think about it, it's really all your fault," she said conversationally, jerking hard on Kara's hair as she spoke. "I mean, if only you'd joined in with the rest of us and taken the pills."

"What's she doing?" Grey mouthed at Izzy. She shook her head. She wanted to concentrate on Mia – to know where this was going. But it was getting harder to hear her. There was a soft buzzing sound starting to creep in at the edge of Izzy's hearing, as though the room was slowly filling with flies… She focused all her attention on the hallway.

"You always have to spoil it, don't you?" Mia was saying. "Always tagging along but never joining in. I mean, it's fine … most of the time. But this time? No."

"I don't understand! Let me go!" Kara groaned.

"Ummm, no. No, I don't think that's going to happen," Mia answered brightly, patting Kara on the head. "You see, you gave Dom the extra pills, didn't you? And then he took them and started getting all paranoid and wanting to tell someone about them…" Her tone darkened. "Can't have that. No. No, no, no, no, no."

She grabbed the back of Kara's head again and smashed her face against the floor, then leaned forward so she could whisper in Kara's ear. "The first time I get even close to being better than my brother and you have to spoil it. *You*." With surprising speed, she jumped off Kara's back, skipping sideways and then kicking her in the ribs. "And now they're all dead because of you."

Kara rolled over and curled into a ball, clutching her ribs and moaning in pain. Mia straightened her T-shirt and glanced down at it, picking a stray hair of Kara's from the front. "And seeing as Tigs was stupid enough to fall off the balcony, I'm going to have to come up with a new plan. Tigs was meant to be the –" she broke off and giggled – "the fall guy. Isn't that funny? She was the fall guy and she fell? You see?" She waited but Kara didn't respond, so she kicked her again. "You're not laughing, Kara. Why aren't you laughing?"

"Because you're *insane*," Kara spat.

Mia laughed. "That'll be the pi-ills!" she said in a sing-song voice. "But like Noah said, that'll wear off. Being dead won't. Awww. Too bad for you." She twirled on the spot. "It's just going to be a pain changing everything to put Izzy in the picture instead of Tigs. I mean, she did at least disappear when I was leading them all round on that merry chase to find Dom, so that's a good start." She put on a little-girl voice and rolled a strand of hair around her fingers. "But Mister Policeman, have you asked Izzy if *she* has an alibi for all those tragic, tragic deaths? I'm afraid she's just come … unhinged. The pressure of a school like Clerkenwell, you see. Not everyone's cut out for it."

Kara had uncurled slightly, and put a hand on the floor in an effort to push herself up. Mia made a tutting sound and stamped on it with her sandal as hard as she could. Kara howled and rolled back into a ball.

"It would have been so much neater with Tigs. I could have left your body here, and when she woke up completely cuckoo, everyone would just have assumed it was all her. Honestly. It's so terribly inconvenient. I thought the sleeping pills were genius. She was so busy shovelling caffeine pills down her throat that she didn't even check the label when I switched them in the cupboard. But then she had to go out on the balcony, didn't she? *God*." Another kick.

Kara was whimpering. Izzy shot a desperate glance at Grey, silently asking him what they could do. He looked back at her blankly, but there were two of them, after all, and only one of Mia. He held up a finger, telling her to get ready…

Mia was sighing and looking down at Kara with

her hands on her hips. "I suppose we're going to have to do something with you," she muttered, glancing over her shoulder as though someone else was talking to her from the living room. "I know, I know!" she said to the imaginary person – and Izzy almost felt a stab of sympathy. Mia was going through exactly the same as the rest of them.

Of course, none of the others had murdered their own brother, their friends, and then tried to frame one of them for it all. Mia had lost it, there was no doubt about that. Whatever she thought about Dom, he was her brother. Her *twin*. There was no way she would ever knowingly hurt him – or at least she wouldn't have *before* she took the pills.

In the hallway, Mia bent down and grabbed another handful of Kara's hair. "Let's just…"

Grey held up his hand, counting off his fingers one at a time. Five … four…

They were going to rush Mia, together.

Three…

Two…

Izzy tensed, getting ready to charge.

Chapter Eighteen

Just as Grey's countdown reached one, there was a shriek. Izzy and Grey looked on as Kara flew up from the floor, hurling herself at Mia and throwing her back along the hallway. The momentum carried them along as far as the biggest bedroom at the end, where they crashed through the door with a combined yell. Izzy and Grey scrambled after them, reaching the door just in time to see them roll out on to the balcony through the open door.

"Kara!" Izzy couldn't stop her shout of warning from exploding out of her mouth.

The scuffle stopped, and both Kara and Mia looked up at them, seeing her in the doorway with Grey behind her. Mia's lip curled into a cold smile as she took advantage of Kara's lapse of concentration and sprang away from her, standing on the balcony like some kind of animal in a cage. Her eyes were wild, staring madly back at them. There was no doubt that she had completely lost her grip on reality — even before her hand snapped forward and grabbed Kara's throat, pulling her close.

Kara eyed them both. Her make-up had smeared across her face and there were streaks of mascara down her cheeks. She looked utterly afraid. The strap of her top was twisted and ripped, and there was a nasty graze on her jaw. Mia's madness had not been kind.

"Izzy! Were your ears burning?" Mia laughed. "We were just talking about you. Well, I was talking. Kara? Mmmm … no. Odd, really. She's usually so … chatty." She shook Kara by the throat for emphasis. "And Grey. Wow. I've got to say, it's a good thing Tigs can't see you looking like that. She'd go right off you. I hate to break it to you, but she was never that interested in your *personality*…" She winked at him. Grey made a low growling sound in the back of his throat.

"Let Kara go. You're done."

"Me? Oh, hardly." She laughed, showing all her teeth. "And besides, Kara's not walking out of here." She winked at Kara, who swayed slightly. "Starting to feel it, are we? You think all that tea I was making you was just for fun? The dose Tigs got was just supposed to knock her out. You … not so much."

She laughed again and Grey snarled. "Let her go!"

"Let her go? What — over there?" Mia yanked Kara closer to the balcony rail. "Sure thing, boss." She pulled and pulled, but Kara resisted. Izzy tried to take a step towards them, but Grey threw his arm out in front of her, stopping her.

"No. Too risky."

"For who?"

"You."

Mia had forced Kara to lean back over the balcony rail. She was alarmingly strong, and Izzy recognized the strength. It was the same strength that had pinned her to the wall beneath Grey's hand. It was the same strength that had smashed up the cars and the door downstairs. It was the same strength that had hoisted Juliet's body on to a meat hook and up into the roof. It was the kind of strength you found when you lost your mind.

Kara's eyes flicked desperately from one to the other of them. She must have seen Izzy's panicked expression. She certainly saw Grey's stern glare at Mia — it showed on her face, just as it showed on

Grey's that he was trying to figure out how to knock Mia away from Kara. A single tear spilled down her cheek, and she took as deep a breath as she could manage with Mia's hand locked round her throat.

"Under the sofa," Kara gasped. "Look under the sofa."

"So you're not completely useless after all, then," Mia said, with a flick of her hair, then she shoved her other hand hard against Kara's chest.

It happened in slow motion – Kara's wobble as she lost her balance, bent achingly far back over the rail. She slipped back, back, back, tipping over and starting to fall. Grey leaped towards the balcony, but it was too late – Kara had gone too far over. But as she fell, her fingers reached up and closed tightly around the top of Mia's arm beneath the soft fabric of her T-shirt. Taken completely by surprise, Mia tipped forward – and in an instant, the two of them had vanished over the edge.

Izzy didn't wait for the sound.

She could see Grey trembling even as he stepped in through the balcony door. "They… She…"

"They fell."

"I wanted to get to her. I wanted… I wanted to…"

"I know."

Her legs gave out beneath her and she slumped to the floor. She needed to cry, but she couldn't. She just felt hollowed-out and empty. The pain that had been building behind her eyes was now a violent headache that made the edges of everything jar. She could barely even lift her hands to push her hair out of her face. All she could think about was lying down on the floor and going to sleep, right where she was. It was close enough to the time now, surely – it had to be. A couple of hours each way couldn't possibly hurt. Not after everything they'd been through.

She lay back on the hard floor. Maybe she didn't even need to sleep; she just needed to rest her eyes for a minute. If she did, the headache might go away.

All she had to do was close her eyes…

"Hey!" The next thing Izzy knew, Grey was shaking her shoulder. "Don't you flake out on me now. Not now, Iz."

"I didn't – did I?" She sat bolt upright. Everything whirled around her as her body tried to keep up with the sudden movement.

"No. You're fine, but it was close enough. I turn my back on you for a second, I look round and you're settling down for a nap. You can't do it, Iz."

"I'm so tired." It came out as a whine.

Grey raised an eyebrow at her. "You're not the only one. I keep wondering whether this is all really a dream and when we're going to wake up."

"Some dream." She knew the feeling. However, she'd also pretty much decided that if it was a dream, there would be a lot more Liam Hemsworth and a lot less dying.

Grey held up a phone and smiled grimly. "I looked under the sofa, like Kara said."

"Whose is it?"

"Kara's. Well, obviously. But she'd left the voice memo running…"

"She taped Mia?"

"Every word. It's been running for ages."

"So, it was definitely all her?" The truth started to sink in. There were no shadowy people chasing them. No one was hunting them down – it was just another one of Noah's conspiracy theories. They were so paranoid from the pills, that they'd swallowed the idea whole, and it had fuelled itself.

Dom's death, Juliet's, Noah's, Tigs's and now Kara's… They had all been Mia.

"She killed Dom?"

"That's what it sounds like to me."

"But *she killed Dom*. She killed her twin brother. What's worth that?"

"Think about it. The pills made her as good as him, at least for the exams. You know what they're... What they *were* like." He corrected himself sadly. "All that teasing each other? Competing over everything? I guess all that, with the pills, made her turn on him."

"And when he started to freak out and threaten to tell someone..."

"He had to go." Grey hung his head. Looking down at himself, he drew a sharp breath in. "We need to leave, Izzy." There was sudden panic in his voice.

"What's the matter?"

"Look at us. We've got blood all over us, and there's three bodies down there on the podium."

"The police."

"Exactly. They're going to be looking for wherever they fell from – and they're going to start pretty high up."

With perfect timing, one of the lifts on the landing pinged.

"We need to not be here," hissed Grey. "This way."

He held his hand out to her, helping her to her feet. He stepped through the door on to the balcony – the exact same place Mia had been standing.

"I can't." Izzy froze to the spot. "It's so high. So high."

"You have to – because any moment now, there are going to be police everywhere. And that's if there aren't already. We have to go now, and this is the only way out." He tugged on her hand, and that was when she realized he was still holding it. "Stay as close to the wall as you can. There might be someone down there, looking up."

Someone hammered on the front door of the apartment. "Did you hear that?" Izzy asked and Grey nodded. "I guess it's real, then."

He gave her a puzzled look. "We're going to follow the balcony round till we get to the fire escape stairs, and then we're going to take them all the way down to the car park."

"The door down there – it's smashed. The lock won't work."

He gave her another look. "We'll cross that one when we get to it, shall we? For now, we just need to not be here."

"But…" Izzy struggled to clear her head. Everything was moving so fast – too fast. Was there any way out of this? "What if we just … told them. If we told the police everything. We could just give them the phone. Maybe they could help? It would be over…"

Another knock on the door.

Grey wasn't listening. Not to her, anyway. He slipped the phone into his pocket. "All right. Let's go."

They made their way along the balcony, peering around the divider to the next apartment. All the curtains were drawn and the doors on to the balcony were closed.

"I think we're good," Grey said, giving the divider a shove. It grated against the concrete, but grudgingly it swung aside. They closed it behind them and padded along the outside of the flat as quickly as they could. At the far end of that side of the tower, a door much like the one to the car park opened into the wall. It wasn't locked – instead, it was fastened with a glass safety bar, which Grey smashed with the side of his fist. "Ladies first," he said, holding it open for her.

A gust of wind rushed up the stairs and through the door as the pressure inside the building shifted. So high up, the slightest breeze whistled through the ventilation shafts and made eerie moaning noises. Izzy peeped over the edge and looked right down the stairwell.

That was a mistake.

Thirty-plus floors of bare concrete stairs spiralled away from her. As she watched, they actually started to spin round and round. Something metallic flashed through the centre of the tower and was gone.

"You OK there?" Grey was waiting for her on the third step.

"Sure," she said weakly. Her problem with heights was on the verge of being A Serious Problem.

"Just don't look down."

"I'm trying not to. It's just that there's such a *lot* of down. It's kind of hard to miss."

"Stick to the wall and you'll be fine." He was trying to be reassuring, but he was starting to sound impatient, too.

"'Fine' is such a loose concept, don't you think?"

"All you've got to do is hold it together a few more hours."

Izzy was so tired. She was somewhere beyond tired. She was even ready to be led down the stairs, one flight at a time, by Grey. She didn't care any more.

She could barely lift her feet. Her tongue felt three sizes too big for her mouth and her eyes had been replaced with small, round stones that someone had left in a fire for a while, then stuffed back into the empty sockets. Her head throbbed more with every step she took, and there was a loud buzzing sound that she could have sworn was a…

A saw.

The metal flash.

As the buzzing sound got louder and louder, she could see Grey talking to her, but she couldn't hear him. And she could see him frowning, watching her, wondering what was wrong and why she had stopped moving. He couldn't see what she could. He couldn't see it, so it couldn't be real. It couldn't be real, could it? But what about the gouges in the walls? They looked real enough, and Izzy was sure that if she touched them, her fingers would catch on the rough edges. What about the dust piled on the edges of the steps where the blade had sliced through concrete and paint and anything else it happened to find in its path? She could almost smell it.

Suddenly, the razor-sharp disc was swinging straight at her. Vicious metal teeth hurtled towards her, spinning first one way and then another – and she had no time to move. It knocked her back, pinning her to the wall. She felt the cold, hard pressure of the blade on her stomach – and felt it tearing its way through her, ripping right out through her side. She tried to cry out but could make no sound. Blood bubbled up into her throat as she reached for Grey, standing helpless on the stairs. He had his back to her now – hadn't seen, hadn't heard. How could he not have heard?

The blade was swinging back, heading straight for him.

No sound came out, no matter how hard she tried. She felt herself sliding down the wall as the saw blade scythed through Grey's shoulder. He dropped to his knees, turning as he fell and crying out. His face twisted in pain and in shock. Their eyes met as the saw came back for another swing.

"Come *on*, Izzy!"

She was jolted out of the trance by Grey calling to her. There he stood, still three steps ahead of her and without a scratch on him. Her hands jumped to her stomach, feeling for the spot where she'd been sliced by the blade. Nothing.

She peeled herself away from the wall and took a couple of unsteady steps down. "I don't think I can take much more of this. I just want it to be over. I don't care any more. I just want it to stop."

"Bad one?" he asked gently.

"You could say that."

"Can't be worse than the yellow line trying to eat you, can it?"

"You want to bet?"

They made their way down the stairs, clinging to the handrail, to the walls, to each other. Every step was a mountain. Every breath was a fight. Izzy lost count of the number of times she stumbled and nearly took the pair of them down. Grey wasn't much better, either; his usually confident step unsteady and unsure. By the time they'd made it down more than thirty floors, all the way to the car park level, her legs were shaking so hard that she couldn't ever imagine feeling steady on them again. Her feet throbbed and her heart sank as she stared at the broken glass in the door.

"I told you. It's broken."

"And how can you be so sure?"

"Because I did it. You know, when I was all woohoo…" She made a corkscrewing motion with her finger alongside her ear.

"You're always woohoo. But you only smashed the one side, didn't you?" Grey pointed to the lock. On this side, it was untouched.

The door opened into the car park.

"Show-off."

"Well, yeah. Let's face it, if I went psycho on a door, at least I'd do it properly."

"You're not helping." Izzy shook her head.

"I'm just trying to hold on to what's left of my mind."

"You and me both," she sighed.

She let him go first. He seemed to know the car park level better than she did – after all, he had lived there longer. He turned sharply right, away from the smashed cars still lurking in the gloom and the faint sound of sirens filtering through from the Beech Street tunnel. It wouldn't be long before the car park was full of police, too – and how long would it take them to put the bodies in Smithfield together with what they found at the bottom of the tower? How long before they found Dom? How long before someone worked out that the one thing all these dead kids had in common was that they went to Clerkenwell. And where would it go from there?

"Shouldn't really come this way," he muttered as he checked around them and put his shoulder to a rusty sheet of metal covering a door. "They're meant to have locked this one down properly, but it's still open. One of the lobby porters showed me once. I think everyone else has forgotten it…"

The sheet of metal fell away to reveal a solid steel door. Both the door handle and lock were missing. In their place was a large strip of rubber, nailed into a loop to make a temporary handle. Judging by how cracked the rubber was, it had been a temporary handle for a very long time. Grey hauled the door open and closed it again after them.

"Where are we?" They had come out into a short corridor. Behind them was a blank wall, in front of them was another glass and steel security door. Everything beyond it was dark. Lining the corridor itself were two rows of what looked like wire mesh cages, each of them just taller than an adult and wide enough for both Grey and Izzy to stand side by side in them.

"Residents' stores," Grey said. "You never been down here?"

"No, I haven't." Izzy peered into one of the cages. It was largely empty, except for a looming circular shape.

"Just a bike," said Grey, holding up Kara's phone. The light from the screen illuminated the inside of the storage locker, proving that it was indeed just a bike balanced on its rear wheel and wedged into the cage.

"The way out?" she asked, pointing at the door. "Where does it go?"

"You'll see."

The door opened on to the steps down to the garden, which gave them a choice between taking the stairs up to the forecourt of Lauderdale, hoping they weren't spotted, or across the garden and round into the back of the tower through the parking levels.

"I know what you're thinking," Grey said with a shrug. "Both suck."

"Yes, they do. They really, really do."

They chose the garden.

Izzy tried to ignore the shadows beneath the bushes. She pretended she didn't see the shape swinging from the branch of the big tree – the one that looked uncannily like a body strung up by its throat. She chose not to look at the darkened windows of Juliet's house as they crept past it. This wasn't how the summer was supposed to go; wasn't how her life was supposed to go. None of it was. And somehow, knowing it was Mia who had done all those things made it worse than if it had been a stranger. Mia, whose apartment they'd all been in. Mia, who was always the one who knew where classes were and would cover for you if you were late. Mia, the organized one. The one who would always have time for you if you had a problem. She'd never let on that she was *that* jealous of Dom. She'd always shrugged off the idea of competing with him or comparing herself to him as a joke – at least, she'd never let on to Izzy that it was anything more.

Maybe Grey had been right. Maybe you never did really know your friends.

They slipped through the garden, and the solid blocks of the Barbican loomed overhead, looking down on them. Lauderdale Tower rose so high above them that it seemed to go on forever, and for a heart-stopping moment Izzy was convinced it was about to topple over and come crashing down right on their heads. She shook the thought away.

The sky was already pink and starting to darken at the edges, and high above, there were fine streaks of orange-purple clouds. How could it be the evening already? Time had taken on a soft, stretchy feel – minutes had turned into hours and hours into seconds. She couldn't tell any more. It was all distorted and wrong.

Wrong. If ever a word could sum up a situation, that was the one. Well. There were others, but they were definitely not the kind of words a Clerkenwell student wanted to be caught using...

She stifled a giggle and Grey stared at her, shocked. "What's so funny?"

"I was just thinking, and then I thought about school ... and then I kind of wondered exactly how all this is going to end. Because, you know, even if they don't find out about the pills, we're still basically the only two left out of all our friends and there are going to be questions and I don't think it makes a whole lot of difference how we answer them because every way you look at it I reckon we're pretty much screwed!" She could hear her voice getting higher and higher until it had taken on the same sing-song tone as Mia's had.

Grey gawped at her – and took a very careful step back. "I think we need to get you home."

The car park level of Lauderdale was as deserted as always, and Izzy was glad that she wasn't there alone. Just in case she got any more secretly destructive urges and decided to take them out on her neighbours' cars with a lump of metal – or, for a bit of variety, tried to kick the windscreens in.

Except suddenly there weren't any cars. And she wasn't in the car park any more.

She was in the lower lift lobby, waiting for the lift with Grey. He was staring at her again.

"What?"

"You."

"Weren't we just in the car park?"

"Yeah, we were. And we walked through and came here, and you started whispering something to yourself and you're really freaking me out."

"But we were…"

"And now we're here, OK?" He poked at the

button again. There was a sign next to one of the lift doors, written in careful block lettering and informing them that lifts two and three would be out of service for the next forty-eight hours. No wonder things were slow.

Izzy read the sign and started to giggle again. "Forty-eight hours," she laughed. "Why's it always forty-eight hours? Is it magic?"

Grey pressed the lift button again. Harder.

At long last, the lift arrived, and it was only as they stepped in that Izzy realized she was chanting "forty-eight, forty-eight, forty-eight" under her breath. She'd had no idea she was doing it. Appalled, she stopped. No wonder Grey had been looking so nervous.

I'm not Mia, she told herself. *I'm not. I'm not.*

And everything looks better after a good night's sleep.

Grey was leaning against the corner of the lift. She could hear his breathing. It was heavier than usual.

Faster than usual.

"Grey?"

He didn't answer. His eyes were closed and his head was tipped back against the metal walls.

"Grey…"

He was breathing faster and harder now, through clenched teeth.

"Grey…"

"No." His voice was ragged.

The lift pinged as it reached her floor. As the doors opened, he shook his head and, without even opening his eyes, he planted a hand on her chest and pushed – hard. She tumbled backwards out of the lift and landed sprawled on the landing as the lift doors closed.

He was going up. Alone.

Frantic, Izzy hammered on the lift 'call' button. Nothing happened. There wasn't a single sound from either of the other lifts – and then she remembered the sign and kicked herself. Only the one lift was working. The lift Grey had taken. There was only one floor he would go to – his own. The eighteenth floor.

She had run away earlier. She had run away from him, and they had both run away from whatever, whoever, they thought had been after them in Smithfield.

No more running away.

As the lift's floor indicator settled on eighteen, Izzy made for the stairs.

Chapter Nineteen

Izzy threw the door to the stairwell open so hard that it smacked back against the wall. The echo boomed all around her.

"Five floors. It's nothing, right?" she told herself, as though it would make each step hurt less. Her bones were on fire inside her, and even the slightest touch pricked her skin sharply. Her clothes felt like she was wearing a porcupine inside out. The feel of her hair brushing against her neck made her want to pull it out by the handful. But she could climb five floors of stairs.

She had to, because somewhere at the top of them was Grey — and there was no way she was going to let him slip away now.

There was just the small problem of what the stairs were doing.

All the steps were moving like funhouse stairs. They tipped at crazy angles, shuffled back and forth and popped up and down.

"You have got to be kidding me."

She stared at them. She knew she just had to convince herself that it wasn't real. That the stairs were really there and they were just normal stairs.

Which was difficult, because several of them were on fire.

She could feel the heat from the flames, could smell burning hair. She could almost hear flesh sizzling and popping behind the crackle of the flames – and that was when she caught herself thinking *almost*. Of course she could *almost* hear it. It wasn't actually there for her to hear.

"All in my head…"

The first step was cold and solid beneath her foot. So was the second, and the third, and the fourth.

"Izzy! Izzy!"

She stopped, clinging on to the handrail. Someone was calling her name over and over.

"Izzy! Izzy! Help me!"

Four steps ahead of her, Tigs was standing on the staircase. She looked so like herself, as though nothing had happened, that Izzy wondered whether she was really there. Whether it had been someone else who fell from the tower. Her hands were folded in front of her and she was watching Izzy intently.

"I asked you to help me. You didn't come."

"I did. I tried, anyway."

"You didn't help me."

"What was I supposed to do?"

"You didn't help me. I needed you."

"I'm sorry. I'm sorry…"

"I fell. I fell, Izzy. All that way and the ground was so hard. You didn't come, and the ground was so hard." Tigs shook her head sadly, and a tear slid down her face. "Why didn't you come? I thought you were my friend."

"I am. I was. I…"

"I told you I was sorry. You said you didn't blame me. I said I was sorry."

"Tigs…"

"You should be sorry. Sorry, sorry, sorry. You *will* be sorry." Tigs took a step forward, then another, then another until she was level with Izzy, nose to nose with her. Izzy blinked as a blanket of exhaustion wrapped around her. She had seen the body fall; had heard Mia say Tigs had fallen. She opened her eyes to find the stairwell empty. She was alone.

She pressed on up the stairs. They seemed to go on forever – first one floor, then another, then another. Three down, two to go.

"Izzy…"

She tried to ignore it. It was Dom, his face pushing out from the concrete wall, stretching it into a mask.

"Izzy! Over here!"

"You're dead, Dom," she replied through gritted teeth. Dom's face vanished, only to reappear higher up the stairs. She could see the wall bulging around his features as they tried to push through.

"See you soon, Izzy."

He vanished again.

She kept on climbing.

Her heart was pounding more heavily than ever and she could hear the blood rushing round her body. It made a faint whooshing, whistling sound. She used the rhythm to push herself up the last few steps. She might as well have been trying to climb the sky – the stairs were impossibly high and steep, towering over her. The door out on to the landing loomed ahead and despite herself, she hesitated in front of it. She was so tired. So, so tired. Her eyes grated in their sockets and she'd almost forgotten what the world was like without the crashing, burning pain in her head. Her hands shook, the palms sticky with sweat. A ball of nausea sat in the pit of her stomach. All she needed was to rest, just for a couple of minutes. If only she could sleep. Just a few minutes.

Everything looks better after a good night's sleep.

What would it be like, anyway? If she gave in, if she went to sleep? Would she still be herself when she woke up, or would she be someone else? Would the part of her that was her, that made her *Izzy,* disappear?

You shouldn't be here, dearie...

What had it felt like to be the man in the video they'd seen? Had he known what he was doing? Was he locked away in the back of his own head, looking out and watching someone else pilot his body, helpless to stop it? Or did he simply not care?

She thought about Mia's laughter.

Worse, had he known exactly what he was doing and liked it?

No, thought Izzy. *No sleep. Not now, not yet.* If she was going to die — and by now, it was looking like the odds of that were pretty good — at least she would die as herself. Not as someone else like Mia had – a twisted version of herself, willing to do anything to win.

She would win by staying Izzy.

It would be nice if she could manage to keep breathing, too.

She pushed open the door.

There was a draught on the landing, and it only took her a moment to understand why. The door to Grey's apartment stood open. She could faintly hear an answerphone message playing on a loop – a beep, and then Grey's mother's voice. The clatter of plates and glasses from a party in the background; laughter. A burst of static, and then her voice again, and then a beep and the whole thing started over again. The door swung gently back and forth in the moving air.

The flow of air was coming from the lift shaft on the far side of the landing. The doors had been forced open. A screwdriver lay discarded on the carpet and there were shreds of metal and rubber littered about the floor.

"Grey? You don't want to be standing there."

He was standing with his back to her, his bare feet already at the edge of the open shaft. His toes stuck out over the drop. His trainers lay at the bottom of the central lift-control console, the laces almost torn out.

"Come back from the edge. Come over here to me." She held a hand out, talking to him in what she hoped was a calm sort of voice. He ignored her.

"Grey, don't."

In the lift shaft, the wind whistled. Grey swayed.

What should she do? What *could* she do? He didn't look like he was going to move, and she had to get him away from the open shaft. Whatever happened after that, she would just have to deal with – but after she got her best friend away from the eighteen (and then some) storey drop.

"Right. I'm going to come over there to you, seeing as you won't come to me. Don't freak out," she added, more to herself than anything else. She trod gently, trying not to make her movements heavy or sudden, talking quietly all the while, her voice soft and low, the way people talk to cornered animals. She said anything that came into her head, anything that might keep him there. She had no idea whether he could hear her or whether he was lost in a world only he could see. She didn't know how long it would last, how deeply he would go into whatever it was he was seeing. She didn't even know whether he would come back at all – as Grey, at least. Nothing was right, nothing was real, but all that mattered was now.

She reached the edge of the shaft and stopped alongside Grey. He was staring at the dark wall on the far side, or at the taut lift cables that stretched down from the top of the building. The emptiness yawned up at them, and Izzy swallowed hard. Her head felt like someone had trapped it in a vice and was squeezing it harder and harder, but she had to keep trying to get through to him.

"I've never seen inside the lift shafts," she said, trying to sound conversational. "They're not all that."

Beside her, Grey's shoulders heaved. Out of the corner of her eye, she could see his chest moving up and down with each breath.

"I mean, I thought they'd at least be encrusted with diamonds or something. Or do you think that's only the lifts in Shakespeare? Tigs said…"

She stopped. She couldn't talk about Tigs. Not now. Her name had just slipped out, unthinkingly. She tried again. "Come away from the edge."

Still nothing.

She tried a different approach. Perkier. Like everything was the way it should be – the way it would have been if only Tigs had never found the pills, if only they'd never taken them, if only they'd told her there was no way they were getting involved, if only… "This is getting so old. Can't we just go to sleep? I just want to sleep."

"So sleep." His voice sounded like it came from the bottom of a deep well.

"Funny." She peered down the shaft. It was a very, very long way down and she very, very much wanted to not be standing so close to it. She could stand next to Grey without standing so close to it. She could.

She tried to step back. She couldn't. There was something stopping her.

It was a hand, pressed flat against the small of her back.

It was Grey's hand.

"Hey!"

He turned his head to look at her, slowly, slowly. And when she realized that his eyes were empty of everything that made him Grey, were flat and cold and steely, and that the grin that was spreading across his face was sharp and cruel – that was when she realized she had made a terrible mistake.

"What's the matter?" He tipped his head to one side and blinked at her. "Don't you want to see what's down there?"

He pressed harder against her lower back, forcing her to lean towards the lift shaft. She tried to push back against him, away from the gaping dark of the shaft. "Get your hand off me."

"You know what's down there? Sleep. Sleep forever. Isn't that what you want? To sleep? You could fall asleep... Get it?" He laughed, and his laugh was empty. "Fall ... asleep. Falling ... asleep. Fall ... asleep. Falling ... asleep."

He sounded horribly like Mia had, his voice just as distant. He even used the same words – was he that far gone? She couldn't bring herself to believe it. Not him. Not Grey.

The lift shaft yawned up at her. Far below in the darkness, a voice was calling her name. Two voices. Three. Her friends' voices, calling her, screaming for her to help them as she balanced on the edge of the drop.

"You don't want to do this," she said, hoping he

wouldn't hear the fear in her voice.

"Don't I?" He nudged her again and she forced herself back before she could lose her balance. "I mean, how do you know? How well do you think you know me?"

"Grey, I *know* you."

"Do you? Are you *sure*?" He narrowed his eyes at her. "How well does anyone ever know their friends?"

Izzy didn't know where he was going with this, but as long as he was talking, she had time to think. And if she had time to think… "I know you well enough. I know that this isn't you."

"Isn't it? You and me, we're the only two left. Imagine how much easier it would be if there was only one left. No one else to worry about. No stories to get straight. Just one story – the only story. And when there's only one story, it becomes the truth, doesn't it?"

"And that story would be yours, would it?" Her heart was pounding so hard that she could feel it in her teeth. There was a way out.

Grey was still talking, but she couldn't make out the words any longer. He might as well have been speaking through cloth.

Only one story, whispered a voice in the back of Izzy's head. *Only one story*.

She could make it hers. She could tell the story. No one needed to know about the pills. No one.

All she had to do was...

No. She shut the voice out. It was Mia's voice, Grey's voice – the fake Izzy's voice. It was the pills. It wasn't her. Not at all.

"My story, my ending," she said as Grey's hand twitched on her back.

It was all she needed.

Chapter Twenty

She threw herself back as hard as she could, dropping all of her weight towards the relative safety of the landing – away from the awful darkness of the shaft and the voices that were still echoing up from inside. The sudden movement took Grey by surprise, and they both tumbled to the floor. Izzy's shoulder twisted beneath her and she fell hard, knocking the air out of her lungs. She gasped for breath, trying to sit up and to get away – to the open apartment door or to the stairs, anywhere.

On the carpet beside her, Grey groaned and shook his head. He had fallen better than she had, but he was just as tired and it looked like he had caught the edge of the lift console with the side of his head. A trickle of blood ran down the side of his jaw from his ear as he lunged at her.

She rolled sideways out of his reach, but he was already on his feet, staggering drunkenly towards her.

He shook his head again – harder this time – as he moved in. Izzy scuttled back as fast as she could, but the floor was too soft and it clung to her hands, sucking them down into the carpet like quicksand. Everything was getting bright, too bright. Grey was moving more slowly, still shaking his head and squinting as though the light hurt his eyes, too.

Time… thought Izzy. *Time. That's all I need…*

With the last of her strength, she pulled herself to her feet and threw herself at him. Again, she surprised him and again she knocked him to the floor. They rolled over and over, away from the shaft, and the taste of something rotten filled her mouth. The lights were getting brighter and there was an itch somewhere in the back of her brain and something was *happening*, and the vice around her skull was tightening, tightening, tightening – squeezing her out of her own head.

They slammed into the wall together – and Izzy stared up into the light. Everything had a gleaming white halo – even the figure leaning over her and closing his hands around her throat.

She wriggled, pulling herself first one way then another, but he was pinning her between his knees and the wall. All she could see was the white light, closing over everything. Swallowing it. Even his face. Her throat burned and she coughed for air, but Grey held firm. She couldn't keep fighting. She was too tired. Too tired to fight Grey. Too tired to fight the other voices in her head. Just too tired. But…

Something was different. Something was changing – she could *feel* it. She could feel the buzz in the back of her head, something she hadn't felt in an age. Something she hadn't felt since the first time she'd taken one of the FokusPro pills. The walls bulged and the lights were blazing overhead, and for a second she saw broken glass and heard a scream, bleeding through from the past into the present – and she was out of air.

Out of air, out of time.

Her fingers wrapped around Grey's, but she might as well have been trying to open a statue's hands. They were strong and cold. So cold. Or was that her. She was cold. She was tired. So tired. So cold.

Just sleep.

She could sleep…

With one last effort, she pushed back against him – and, miraculously, Grey's hands dropped away from her neck. The world snapped back into focus as air rushed into her lungs. She gasped, gulping it down as hard and as fast as she could, tensing herself for whatever was coming.

It never came. He was sitting in front of her, his back against the centre console, blinking groggily.

"We were on the steps…" he started, then stopped and blinked at her again. He kept glancing down at his hands as though he didn't quite understand what they had been doing. "We were on the steps, Iz."

"We're not on the steps now," she managed. The words grated her throat.

"No." He swallowed loudly, holding his hands up in front of his face. They were shaking. "I'm sorry, Izzy. I'm so, so sorry. I didn't know. I couldn't… I wasn't…" He hung his head. "What did I do?"

He didn't remember.

He couldn't remember.

One story. When there's only one story, it becomes the truth.

He doesn't need to remember.

My story. My ending.

She'd made bad choices before. Wrong choices. Choices made because she was afraid and because she wanted to win, and choices that did more damage than they did good. Not this time.

She wasn't afraid any more. It made everything so much easier. So much clearer.

She could choose again, and she could choose right.

She rolled on to her side and slid her back up the wall. She felt like she'd been hit by a truck, and then reversed over. Twice.

"Nothing, Grey. You're OK – you didn't do anything."

"But … I…" He held up his hands, unable to bring himself to say any more.

"You were standing by the lift shaft, and it scared me. I … kind of tackled you out of the way."

"You did?"

"Yeah. Sorry about that." She thought she'd try getting up from the floor. It didn't go so well. She sat down again.

"Then what?"

"Then nothing. We fell, you landed on me, you moved. Ta-da." She waved her hands weakly.

Grey narrowed his eyes and looked her up and down, but what could he say?

Izzy had made her choice.

Grey rolled on to his back, groaning. "You know," he said, reaching a hand out towards her, "maybe you and me … us… Maybe we should go out sometime."

"What makes you say that?"

"Because how could any first date be worse than this?"

Izzy looked at his hand. The hand that had been around her throat, cutting off her oxygen. He could have killed her. He almost had.

But had that been Grey, or was it the version of Grey that the pills had created. And what if, deep down, the two weren't all that different?

Had it been Mia, the real Mia, who had killed the others, or had that been down to the pills, too? Had they pushed her so far over the edge that she was prepared to kill all of them, even her own brother, just for the sake of being the best... Or was she so desperate to be the favourite, to be better than Dom, that she would do whatever it took to keep her method a secret?

It couldn't possibly have been the real Izzy who had smashed up all those cars.

You shouldn't be here, dearie…

After all, it wasn't like she'd done anything like that before — was it?

Not that anyone could prove, anyway; never mind what her old teacher had said. That was what saved her. Not from getting expelled, obviously, or from the hours and hours of therapy designed to "get her back to a good place, emotionally". But it had saved her from the police or social services and … the rest of it. Besides, she was a good student, wasn't she? A dedicated student, even if she maybe wasn't the smartest in the class. And that's why she'd cracked under the pressure — she'd simply wanted it more.

Two grade points. That's all she'd asked for. The difference between a pass and a fail. She'd asked for a re-mark, she'd begged. And the teacher had folded her arms and turned her down flat. Izzy had never felt anger like that before — sheer rage at the injustice of it. It wasn't even like her answer on the paper had been wrong. Just not clear enough. It wasn't fair. She'd worked so hard and done her best and then… Then someone was telling her that her best simply wasn't good enough.

"You shouldn't be here, dearie…" A teacher's

concern for a teenage girl all alone in a deserted car park after dark.

A teacher who didn't spot the metal bar in Izzy's hand as she walked away and who, when she turned the corner to her parking space, could barely believe that *anyone* – let alone Izzy – could do *that* to her car...

Izzy looked over at Grey's outstretched hand. He blinked at her. "You and me," he said again, and tried to sit up, before groaning and flopping back down on to the floor.

"I guess I'm staying here for a while." He rubbed his hands through his hair. "How'd the lift doors get like that, anyway?"

"Maintenance must have left them at the end of their shift, I suppose. Not exactly safe," Izzy said, kicking the screwdriver he'd used to prise open the doors out of the way. He didn't need to know, did he?

"And my shoes? What's that about?"

She forced a smile. "I didn't want to bring it up. I thought it was some kind of hippy statement," she said weakly, and held up a hand. It was scratched and bruised, and still stained red. "I'm thinking … hospital?"

"You're sure you want to do that?"

"They're dead, Grey. All our friends are gone. Sooner or later, it's all going to come out – everything that's happened. But we're still here, and we need to be OK."

"We're going to be OK, Iz. I promise." He smiled at her, and his face lit up in a way she'd never seen before – or at least never noticed. He reached out for her hand again.

"I hope so," she said, smiling back. And as her fingers twined through his, the backs of their hands brushed the carpet – and something cold lying there in the middle of the floor. Something metal. Something sharp.

Izzy felt Grey's fingers tighten around hers – or was it hers tightening around his? One of them was holding the other so tightly that the bones in her hand were starting to ache, but it was impossible to tell who. Her eyes locked with Grey's and as one, they turned their gazes towards the object lying on the floor between them.

We can't just leave it there, can we? Anything could happen to it.

Izzy's scar throbbed painfully as the scalpel glittered in the light – and as the smile on Grey's face faded, Izzy found herself starting to giggle...

Turn the page to read an extract from

FROZEN CHARLOTTE

ISBN: 978-1-84715-840-6

RED EYE

An extract from *Frozen Charlotte*
by Alex Bell

When Jay said he'd downloaded a Ouija-board app on to his phone, I wasn't surprised. It sounded like the kind of daft thing he'd do. It was Thursday night and we were sitting in our favourite greasy spoon café, eating baskets of curly fries, like always.

"Do we have to do this?" I asked.

"Yes. Don't be a spoilsport," Jay said.

He put his phone on the table and loaded the app. A Ouija board filled the screen. The words YES and NO were written in flowing script in the top two corners, and beneath them were the letters of the alphabet in that same curling text, in two arches. Beneath that was a straight row of numbers from zero to nine, and underneath was printed GOODBYE.

"Isn't there some kind of law against Ouija boards or something? I thought they were supposed to be dangerous."

"Dangerous how? It's only a board with some letters and numbers written on it."

"I heard they were banned in England."

"Couldn't be, or they wouldn't have made the app. You're not scared, are you? It's only a bit of fun."

"I am definitely *not* scared," I said.

"Hold your hand over the screen then."

So I held out my hand, and Jay did the same, our fingertips just touching.

"The planchette thing is supposed to spell out the answers to our questions," Jay said, indicating the little pointed disc hovering at one corner of the screen.

"Without us even touching it?"

"The ghost will move it," he declared.

"A ghost that understands mobile phones? And doesn't mind crowds?" I glanced around the packed café. "I thought you were supposed to play with Ouija boards in haunted houses and abandoned train stations."

"That would be pretty awesome, Sophie, but since we don't have any boarded-up lunatic asylums or whatever around here, we'll just have to make do with what we've got. Who shall we try to contact?" Jay asked. "Jack the Ripper? Mad King George? The Birdman of Alcatraz?"

"Rebecca Craig," I said. The name came out without my really meaning it to.

"Never heard of her. Who did she kill?"

"No one. She's my dead cousin."

Jay raised an eyebrow. "Your what?"

"My uncle who lives in Scotland, he used to have another daughter, but she died when she was seven."

"How?"

I shrugged. "I don't know. No one really talks about it. It was some kind of accident."

"How well did you know her?"

"Not that well. I only met her once. It must have been right before she died. But I always wondered how it happened. And I guess I've just been thinking about them again, now that I'm going to stay in the holidays."

"OK, let's ask her how she died. Rebecca Craig," Jay said. "We invite you to speak with us."

Nothing happened.

"Rebecca Craig," Jay said again. "Are you there?"

"It's not going to work," I said. "I told you we should have gone to a haunted house."

"Why don't *you* try calling her?" Jay said. "Perhaps she'll respond to you better. You're family, after all."

I looked down at the Ouija board and the motionless planchette. "Rebecca Craig—"

I didn't even finish the sentence before the disc started to move. It glided smoothly once around the board before coming back to hover where it had been before.

"Is that how spirits say hello, or just the app having a glitch-flip?" I asked.

"Shh! You're going to upset the board with your negativity. Rebecca Craig," Jay said again. "Is that you? Your cousin would like to speak with you."

"We're not technically—" I began, but the planchette was already moving. Slowly it slid over to YES, and then quickly returned to the corner of the board.

"It's obviously got voice-activation software," I said. With my free hand I reached across the table to pinch one of Jay's fries.

He tutted at me, then said, "Spirit, how did you die?"

The planchette hovered a little longer this time before sliding over towards the letters and spelling out: B-L-A-C-K

"What's that supposed to mean?" I asked.

"It's not finished," Jay replied.

The planchette went on to spell: S-A-N-D

"Black sand?" I said. "That's a new one. Maybe she meant to say quicksand? Do they have quicksand in

Scotland?"

"Spirit," Jay began, but the planchette was already moving again. One by one, it spelled out seven words:

D-A-D-D-Y

S-A-Y-S

N-E-V-E-R

E-V-E-R

O-P-E-N

T-H-E

G-A-T-E

"It's like a Magic Eight ball," I said. "It just comes out with something random each time."

"Shh! It's not random, we're speaking with the dead," Jay said, somehow managing to keep a straight face, even when I stuck my tongue out at him. "Is that why you died, spirit?" he asked. "Because you opened the gate?"

The planchette started to move again, gliding smoothly around the lighted screen:

C-H-A-R-L-O-T-T-E

I-S

C-O-L-D

"Charlotte?" I said. "I thought we were speaking to Rebecca?"

"Is your name Charlotte?" Jay asked.

The planchette moved straight to NO.

"Are you Rebecca Craig?" I asked.

The planchette did a little jump before whizzing over to YES. And then:

C–H–A–R–L–O–T–T–E

I–S

C–O–L–D

C–O–L–D

C–H–A–R–L–O–T–T–E

I–S

C–O–L–D

C–H–A–R–L–O–T–T–E

I–S

C–O–L–D

"This ghost has a pretty one-track mind," I said with a yawn. "I hope you didn't pay a lot of money for this rubbish? Aren't you supposed to be saving up for a new bike?"

"Yes, but I hate saving money – it's so boring. Maybe I'll get a unicycle instead. Do you think that would make me more popular at school?"

I laughed. "Only if you went to clown school. You'd fit right in there. Probably make Head Boy."

"Head Boy, wouldn't that be something? My mum would die of pride." Jay looked down at the board and said, "You know, some people think that spirits can see into the future. Let's give it a little test. Rebecca, am I ever going to grow another couple of inches taller?"

I giggled as the planchette whizzed around, apparently at random.

N-E-V-E-R

E-V-E-R

O-P-E-N

T-H-E

G-A-T-E

D-A-D-D-Y

S-A-Y-S

D-A-D-D-Y

S-A-Y-S

T-H-E

G-A-T-E

N-E-V-E-R

E-V-E-R

"Do you think I should take that as a 'no'?" Jay asked me.

"Absolutely. Titch for life."

Jay pretended to recoil. "Geez, you don't have to be vicious about it." He looked back down at the board. "Spirit, am I going to pass that maths quiz tomorrow?"

B-L-A-C-K

S-A-N-D

F-R-O-Z-E-N

C-H-A-R-L-O-T-T-E

F-R-O-Z-E-N

S-A-N-D

B-L-A-C-K

C-H-A-R-L-O-T-T-E

C-O-L-D

H-E-R-E

D-A-D-D-Y

Jay and I were both giggling now, like little kids, but his next, and final, question made the laugh stick in my throat. "When will I die?"

This time the planchette gave a different answer. It whizzed around the board aimlessly once again before clearly spelling out seven letters:

T-O-N-I-G-H-T

"I don't think this ghost likes me very much," Jay said, lifting his eyes to mine. "What do you think?"

But before I could respond, we both jumped as a

tinkly, music-box style tune started to play from Jay's phone.

"Is that your new ringtone?" I asked.

"I've never heard it before," Jay replied.

"Now you're just messing with me."

He shook his head and gave me his best innocent look. "It must be part of the app. To make it more spooky."

A girl's voice started to sing – plaintive and childish, high-pitched and wobbly. It was a simple, lilting melody full of melancholy, a song made for quiet campfires, lonely hills and cold nights:

Now Charlotte lived on the mountainside,
In a bleak and dreary spot.
There was no house for miles around,
Except her father's cot.

"You are such a wind-up," I said, smiling and giving Jay's arm a shove. The sing-song voice was starting to get us dirty looks from the other customers in the café. "You put that on there yourself!"

"I swear I didn't," Jay replied. "It's just a really cool app."

"*Such a dreadful night I never saw,*
The reins I scarce can hold."

Fair Charlotte shivering faintly said,
"I am exceedingly cold."

Jay tapped the screen to turn it off but, though the voice stopped singing, the Ouija-board screen wouldn't close. The planchette started spinning around the board manically.

"Dude, I think that app has broken your phone," I said.

It was only a joke. I didn't really think there was anything wrong with the phone that turning it off and on again wouldn't fix, but then the screen light started to flicker, and all the lights in the café flickered with it.

Jay and I looked at each other and I saw the first glimmer of uncertainty pass over his face.

And then every light in the café went out, leaving us in total darkness.

There were grumblings and mutterings from the other customers around us and, somewhere in the room, a small child started to cry. We heard the loud crash of something being dropped in the kitchen.

The only light in the room came from the glow of Jay's mobile phone, still on the table between us. I looked at it and saw the planchette fly over to number nine and then start counting down through the numbers. When it got to zero, someone in the café screamed, a high, piercing screech that went on and on.

Cold clammy fingers curled around mine as Jay took my hand in the darkness and squeezed it tight. I could hear chairs scraping on the floor as people stood up, demanding to know what was happening. More children started to cry, and I could hear glasses and things breaking as people tried to move around in the dark and ended up bumping into tables. And above it all was the piercing sound of a woman crying hysterically, as if something really awful was happening to her.

I let go of Jay's hand and twisted round in my seat, straining my eyes into the darkness, desperately trying to make sense of what was happening. Now that my eyes had adjusted, I could just make out the silhouettes of some of the other people in the café with us – plain black shapes, like shadow puppets dancing on a wall.

But one of them was taller than all the others, impossibly tall, and I realized that whoever it was must be standing on one of the tables. They weren't moving, not at all. Everyone else in the café was moving, even if only turning their heads this way and that, but this person stood completely stock-still. I couldn't even tell if I was looking at their back or their front – they were just staring straight ahead, arms by their sides.

"Do you see that?" I said, but my voice got lost amongst all the others. I stood up and took half a step forwards, staring through the shadows. I could just make out the outline of long hair and a skirt. It was a girl standing on the table in the middle of all this chaos. No one else seemed to have noticed her.

"Jay—" I began, turning back towards him at the exact moment his mobile phone died. The screen light flickered and then went off. At the same time, the café lights came back on. I spun back round to look at the table where the girl had been standing, but there was no one there. The table was empty.

"Did you see her?" I asked Jay.

"See who?"

I stared around for the girl in a skirt, but there was no sign of her.

Anyone would think there'd been an earthquake

or something. There was broken china and glass all over the floor of the café, many of the chairs had fallen over and a couple of tables had overturned.

"Who was that screaming?" people were saying.

"What's happened?"

"Is someone hurt?"

"What the hell is going on?"

"Oh my God, someone's been burnt!"

Bill, the owner, had led one of the waitresses out from the kitchen. She must have been the one who'd screamed in the dark. She was still sobbing and it was obvious why – all the way up her right side she was covered in burns. Her hand, arm, shoulder and the right side of her face were completely covered in a mess of red and black bleeding flesh, so charred that it was hard to believe it had once been normal skin. Her hair was still smoking and the smell made me want to gag.

I heard someone on their phone calling an ambulance as other people moved forward, asking what had happened.

"I don't know," Bill said. He'd gone completely white. "I don't know how it happened. When the lights went out, she must have tripped or something.

I think… I think she must have fallen against the deep-fat fryer…"

I could feel the blood pounding in my ears and turned back round to Jay. Wordlessly, he held up his mobile phone for me to see. From the top of the screen to the bottom there was a huge crack running all the way down the glass.

"Did you… Did you drop it?" I asked.

But Jay just shook his head.

The ambulance arrived soon after that and took the weeping girl away.

"In all the years this place has been open we've never had an accident like this," I heard Bill say. "Never."

Bill went to the hospital with the girl and the café closed early. Everyone filed away, going out to their cars and driving off. Soon, Jay and I were the only ones left. Normally, he would have cycled home and I would have waited by myself for my mum to pick me up but, today, Jay said he would wait with me, and I was grateful to him for that.

"Thanks," I said. "And thanks for holding my hand when the lights went out."

He gave me a sharp look. "I didn't hold your hand."

A prickly feeling started to creep over my skin.

"Yes, you did."

"Sophie, I didn't. You must have... You must have imagined it. It was pretty crazy in there."

I thought of those cold fingers curling around mine and shook my head. "Someone was definitely holding my hand when it went dark," I said. "And if it wasn't you, then who was it?"

"Well, it wasn't me. Maybe you've got a secret admirer."

"Did you see that girl standing on the table? I thought I saw her outline there in the dark."

Jay stared at me. "Are you actually trying to scare me right now? Because it's not going to work, you know. I'm not that gullible."

I glanced back through the windows of the café. There'd been no time to tidy up before the ambulance arrived and the place had been shut up as it was, with tables and chairs and broken crockery everywhere. A couple of the tables looked fairly normal, with plates of untouched food still on them, which was almost weirder.

I shivered and turned away, not wanting to look too closely in case I saw the girl among the empty tables.